DAWN OF THE JADE EMPRESS

AN AIRSHIP DRAGONS PREQUEL

AMY CAMPBELL

Legend Has It LLC

This is a work of fiction. Names, characters, places, and incidents are the product of the author's imagination or are used fictitiously. Any resemblance to actual persons, living or dead, events, or locales is entirely coincidental.

DAWN OF THE JADE EMPRESS

Copyright © 2023 Amy Campbell

All rights reserved. No part of this book may be reproduced or used in any manner without written permission of the copyright owner except for the use of quotations in a book review.

Published in the United States by Amy Campbell

ISBN-13:978-1-957816-96-8

First edition: October 2023

10 9 8 7 6 5 4 3 2 1

www.amycampbell.info

v090723

CHAPTER ONE

The agonized squeal of an injured dragon split the air. Belen's head snapped up as she sunned herself on a cliff. She knew that voice. Rising, she scanned the area below, eyes narrowing when she caught the glimmer of her sister's sky blue scales.

Chandra was pinned by a hardscale dragon nearly three times her size. The bully's scales were jet black with hints of deep purple. He loomed over her, tail lashing as he snarled at the smaller dragon.

"Chandra!" Belen shouted, her voice echoing through the canyon. She launched from the cliff and glided towards them with deadly intent in her eyes, claws extended. "Leave her alone, Kaltik!"

The bully spun around to face Belen, his eyes widening in surprise at the sudden appearance of another dragon. He tried to puff himself up, making himself look larger than he really was to intimidate her, but Belen didn't flinch—instead, she readied herself for battle.

"Stay out of this, Belen. This doesn't concern you," Kaltik growled.

"Chandra is my clutch-sister, so it *does* concern me," Belen shot back, mantling her emerald wings. The black dragon outweighed her, too, but she stood a better chance than her sister. Not only was Chandra small, but her vision was poor. She could barely see past the tip of her snout. "If you harm her, you'll face a reckoning with me."

Kaltik's claws tightened on Chandra's neck. The blue dragon gasped for breath, a bead of crimson blooming beneath her attacker's claws. "Wait. What if we can come to some sort of compromise?" Chandra's voice was a pained rasp.

Belen hesitated, still poised for battle, but Chandra continued speaking. "It doesn't have to be a fight—we can both get something out of this if we work together!"

"There is no compromise," Kaltik rumbled, tail coiling like a snake. "You're an abomination. Dragons aren't meant to have magic."

Ah, so that was what this was about. Like the others, Belen wasn't comfortable with her sister's newfound power, but she wasn't going to turn her back on family. But magic or not, Chandra had a canny mind. She flicked a glance at her sister. "What do you propose?"

"I said no compromise!" The black dragon bared his fangs.

"Then you will die," Chandra whispered, certainty in her voice.

At her pronouncement, Kaltik hesitated, his ear-flaps flattening. "What? Is that a threat?"

He loosened his grip on Chandra. She shook her head sadly, as if the news grieved her. "No, it's a promise. But if you let me up now, you will live."

The bully relaxed his grip, scuttling away. "Stay out of my way, you star-crossed albatross." He tossed a glare at Belen to include her in the insult, then launched into the sky in a thrashing of broad wings.

Once Kaltik was away, Chandra slowly clambered to her feet. She shook out her wings, sighing. "Thank you."

Belen nudged the azure dragon gently. "Are you hurt?"

"Nothing that won't heal soon enough." Chandra squinted at her sister. "You would have fought him for me?"

Belen shrugged. "I think we could take him together. We're both much smarter than he is." The larger hardscale dragons weren't known for their wit. "Did you see a vision of his death? Is that why you told him that?"

Chandra chuckled. "I told him he would die. I didn't say when, however. Everyone dies, some day. It wasn't a lie."

Oh, her sister was a wily thing. Belen grinned at her. "Well played."

"I wish the others thought of me as you do." Chandra lifted a claw, gingerly rubbing at the marks on her tender neck. The blue dragon shivered.

"Kaltik's skull is full of rocks," Belen huffed.

Chandra gave her a gentle nudge. "You're so kind and brave, Belen. I wish everyone could see that."

The azure dragon's eyes narrowed as she looked off into the distance, as if searching for something beyond her physical sight. When she finally spoke again, her voice was soft but determined. "Belen, I have seen a vision of our future." She paused, gathering her courage before finishing the sentence. "I saw you become the Jade Empress—but at a great cost to yourself."

Belen froze. Never had such an honor crossed her mind, but... "What? Me? The Jade Empress? How is that possible?"

"It is only possible if you are willing to sacrifice your own heart," Chandra said solemnly. "Your path will be painful, and you will have to make choices that no one should ever have to make. But if you do, history itself will be changed forever."

At the pronouncement, Belen stiffened. Was a declaration like this what had set off Kaltik? Chandra needed to guard her words. "Are you certain of this?"

Chandra shut her eyes, her tail twitching as the sound of birdsong filled the gap of silence. After a moment, she nodded. "When the visions come, they're as plain as day. Not all of them are so...certain. But this one..." She swallowed.

"It is," Belen finished for her.

"Yes."

"And what is your part in this?" Belen asked.

Chandra arched her neck, unwilling to meet her sister's gaze. "I'm destined to become the Seer. I'll receive a summons to the Vault of Fate within the next three full moons."

A chill threaded down Belen's sinuous spine. Chandra's word choice mattered. Not just a Seer, but *the* Seer. A dragon Seer had lived on the isle of the Vault of Fate for the last two centuries, ever since the disaster that had spread the taint of magic across the world. It was rare for a hardscale dragon to have magic—that was normally relegated to the smaller drakes.

"I suppose the Seer is very old," Belen murmured uneasily. "But Chandra, you don't have to leave the Cerulean Court." She wanted to beg her sister to stay. Chandra was the closest thing she had to a friend.

A sad smile tugged at the corners of Chandra's lips. "I do."

"What happens if you stay?" Belen challenged.

Chandra sighed. "Something worse."

"Worse than what?"

The blue dragoness lowered her head. "You don't want to know."

CHAPTER TWO

The Jade Empress. Belen couldn't stop thinking of Chandra's vision. Was it possible for her to rise to such a position?

She and Chandra were not the whelps of the Cerulean royalty. Each Dragon Court was led by an Emperor and Empress, who ruled their home island. Courtiers were attached to each Court, tasked with protecting their island and migrating in search of the precious ore and gems needed to keep the hardscale dragons in top condition. Younger dragons couldn't withstand the rigors of the migration, so until they reached maturity they remained on their home island, awaiting the return of the older dragons with the precious nutrients.

Belen was on the wing for her first migration as she mulled over her thoughts of Chandra's words. She should have been reveling in the ecstasy of her first migration as an adult, but here she was, befuddled by her sister's vision.

And not only that...*missing* her sister.

As foretold, the Seer had tapped Chandra before migration

season began. The blue dragoness had flown off to the Vault of Fate to begin her training in earnest.

Belen tried to assure herself that she was happy for Chandra. With her low vision, her sister would never have been able to complete a migration. She would have been forced to stay on Cerulean Cove with the Emperor, Empress, and a handful of guards to watch over the fledglings.

She shook her head to clear her mind. *I need to concentrate on the migration!* Belen had almost lagged too far behind the dragon she had been following, which would have spelled disaster. Her instinct told her to go north, but little more than that.

The dragon ahead of her dipped lower in the sky, eventually wheeling down toward an island where Belen noticed other dragons had gone to rest. She approached warily, noting that some of the largest dragons were bickering over the carcass of a whale that an apex-class dragon had hauled ashore.

Others had discovered a grove of dragon fruit, falling upon the bounty with glee. Belen abstained from joining them—dragon fruit had a hallucinogenic effect on dragons, and she wanted to keep a clear mind.

Belen made it a point to steer clear of the more aggressive hardscales, focusing on the nearby trees full of ripe fruit. A few other dragons had made the same decision, and before long, they were gnawing on mangoes beneath the shade of a stand of palms.

"Is this your first time?" one dragon, a female with purple scales, asked Belen by way of greeting.

"Yes." Belen tucked her tail around her feet and introduced herself, eyeing a lovely golden mango. She plucked it from the tree before anyone else could deny her.

The purple nodded. "I'm Kya of the Crimson Court and this

is Sivarth." She lifted a claw toward the red dragon, who sat opposite her.

"Jade Court," Sivarth supplied, tossing aside a mango seed. He paused, sharp fangs worrying at the skin of a fresh mango. "Have you heard the news?"

Kya's eyes widened, and she leaned in. "What news?" She went still, as if she feared any movement would dissuade the red dragon from sharing his gossip.

"Prince Gideon's former consort died. Jade Court will select a new consort when we return from migration." Sivarth's jaws slid into a lopsided grin.

Belen stared. The Jade Court... *By the winds, is Chandra right?* But the consort had *died*. That was alarming. "How did she die?"

Sivarth glanced from side to side, conspiratorial. "The Emperor insists it was natural causes. But rumor has it she was murdered."

Kya shivered. "Who would murder a consort?"

"A rival," Sivarth supplied automatically.

Belen wasn't as certain. Oh, how she wished Chandra was here. They could have found a cozy thicket to sit and bandy about ideas. Something about this wasn't right. But by the same token...this was her chance. *I could really be the Jade Empress.*

"How would a dragoness put her name in contention for the honor?" Belen asked.

The red dragon gave her an assessing look. "You're little more than a whelp. I don't know if you have the experience Gideon will be looking for."

Belen bristled. "This may be my first migration, but I'm not some soft-shell whelp. I can hold my own." She lifted her chin, defiant. Her emerald scales gleamed in the shade-dappled sunlight.

"Hmm." Sivarth traded a glance with Kya. "I suppose everyone deserves a fair shot. After you drop off the ore and gems from your treasure gullet, you would need the permission of your Emperor or Empress. Then simply bring a token to signify their blessing. Something green, preferably."

As a green dragon, Belen thought *she* might be token enough, but there was wisdom in the advice. She nodded. "I appreciate the information. I'll recall your kindness when I'm the Jade Empress."

Sivarth laughed. "I admire your confidence!"

Belen smiled, a mostly polite baring of fangs. He had no idea. She was about to speak when a distant rumble interrupted her. Belen's head swung around, seeking the disturbance. She tensed at the sight of a bulbous dark speck on the horizon.

"What is that?" she whispered.

Kya followed her gaze, though the purple dragon merely flicked the tip of her tail, unconcerned. "Nothing to worry about. A human contraption. They think they've mastered the sky." She snorted derisively.

Belen frowned. "What is it called?"

"The Jade Court has taken to calling them sky whales," Sivarth rumbled. "Though they're rather shy of dragons. If we come near, they turn tail and flee."

"As they should," Kya said. "We are the masters of the sky."

Belen nodded. And nothing would ever take that way.

CHAPTER THREE

The rest of Belen's first migration was uneventful. She accompanied Kya and Sivarth to the continent. The dragons found mines that humans had blasted into the mountains, eating or running off any humans who dared get in their way as they foraged.

As a young dragon, Belen had consumed her share of precious metals and gems to help harden her scales. But those had always been straight from the treasure gullet of another dragon. To rip open the side of a mine shaft in search of the delectable emeralds she sensed nearby...it was a seductive sensation. Empowering.

And even better was the honey-sweet taste of those same gems on her tongue. The more she ate, the tougher her scales became and the stronger she felt.

But the weather turned cooler, the signal for Belen and the others to migrate back to the warm Dragon Latitudes. With her appetite for metal sated and her scales glowing, Belen's treasure gullet brimmed with loot for the young ones. She flew back to the Cerulean Court triumphant.

Belen followed the line of other migrating dragons to the metal larder. As she waited in line to deposit the contents of her gullet, her thoughts turned to Chandra. She missed her sister's steadying presence. But in the same thought, Belen's mind turned to the blue dragon's dire prediction.

"I shape my own destiny. I will not succumb to fate," Belen murmured. The dragon before her in line, a matronly yellow, peered over her wing at the younger dragoness. "Um, sorry, just talking to myself."

Belen clamped her jaw to hide her embarrassment as the yellow turned away. She blew out a frustrated breath. *I have no reason to be embarrassed. One day I'll be an Empress. All I have to do is approach my own Emperor and Empress.*

The Cerulean Court was abuzz with excitement as Belen made her way through the knots of gossiping dragons. Everywhere she went, dragons chattered about the upcoming selection process for the next Jade Consort.

Belen sucked in a steadying breath. *I can do this.* Keeping her spine straight, she strode toward the mouth of the tunnel that led to the chamber of the monarchs. A guardian dragon bobbed his head in greeting, but otherwise let her pass unchallenged.

Emperor Maheer and Empress Malvika reclined on a sumptuous rug in the middle of the cavern. They weren't alone—courtiers ringed the cave, necks arched as the intimate groups gossiped. The royal couple looked up at the sound of Belen's claws on the stone. Malvika's ear-flap twitched in surprise.

"Ah, my niece returns from her first migration. I hope you fared well." Malvika aimed an indulgent smile at her.

Belen lowered her head in deference, extending her forelegs into a bow. "It was an adventure, Empress. But I've come with a request. I wish to be considered for the role of Jade

Consort." Belen swallowed. She didn't know what would come next, and she feared rejection.

The Emperor and Empress exchanged glances before Maheer spoke. "You are young, Belen. What makes you think you could fulfill such a task?"

Belen took a deep breath, as if the air could give her the courage for what she was about to say. It was a speech she had mentally rehearsed on her journey back, a sum of all her thoughts. "My travels have taught me much about the dragons of this court, as well as other courts across the latitudes. I'm not a whelp anymore. I've grown, matured, and realized what my assumption of this role could mean for us." She paused before continuing, choosing her words with care. "I bring more than just my heart to the table. I bring determination and an iron will, which are necessary as consort."

Malvika gave her a fond look. "Niece of mine, I know you speak the truth." She scraped her claws against the stone floor, a nervous gesture. "But word has come to us that Gideon's former consort died under mysterious circumstances. And I would never wish harm to fall upon you." The conversation snared the attention of the courtiers around the chamber, their glowing eyes intent on the delicious conversation.

Belen stiffened, Chandra's prophecy heavy on her mind. She pushed all thoughts of it aside. "The former consort was from the Amber Court. We Ceruleans are made of sterner stuff!" At her declaration, the nearby dragons lifted their voices into a rousing roar. Belen smiled to herself, waiting for the clamor to wane before continuing. "And I ask to do this not for my own benefit, but for that of the Cerulean Court and all dragons."

Maheer sighed. Belen knew she had them. The mixing of bloodlines among the Courts was critical to the continuation of their species. Every year, a handful of young males and females were exchanged between the courts. But to have a consort for another Court selected from among the Ceruleans? It would be a powerful boon.

And as far as Belen knew, no other dragoness had stepped forward.

"We can't deny that this would benefit every dragon who calls Cerulean Cove home," Maheer said after a moment, his gaze drifting across the assembled dragons. Likely hoping that another candidate might step forward. But no one did. Belen knew that the majority of her Ceulean brethren were lazy and disliked change. "You have our blessing."

Malvika nodded, then held up a claw to signal for Belen to wait. The Empress rose, making her way into the dark recesses of the connected chamber she and Maheer called home. She returned a moment later, clutching a golden chain in her claws.

"A gift to grant you luck," Malvika whispered, slipping the chain over Belen's horns and onto her neck.

It rested against Belen's breastbone, and though it was light, it still felt as if it had a strange weight to it. Something she couldn't quite discern. "What is it?"

The Empress glanced askance to make sure no one was near enough to hear her murmured words. "It's a magical item, crafted by a drake. An item with the power to let you understand the speech of any other race, and they, in turn, will understand you."

Belen shivered at the mention of magic. It was anathema to a dragon. Was her aunt giving her a curse, or was this truly an act of kindness? Belen gritted her teeth. Whatever it was, she had to feign grace in this moment. "Your kindness knows no bounds, Empress."

Malvika dipped her horned head. "And before you set out,

fill your gullet with jade and emerald. Green gems from an emerald dragon. *That* should impress the Jade Court."

Perhaps the necklace wasn't a show of bad faith after all. Belen smiled. "As you say." She bowed before the Cerulean Empress, vowing that this was the last time any of the Cerulean Court would see her bow to anyone.

CHAPTER FOUR

Jadefire Island bustled with activity. The scales of hundreds of dragons glimmered under the early afternoon sun. Belen swallowed, less confident than she had been previously. It had been easy to assure herself that she was the best choice to be consort as she had flown here, but now that she was on the island, surrounded by so many unfamiliar dragons...it was another thing altogether.

Counting the Jades, there were six Courts in all. While the Ceruleans had only sent Belen, the Pearls, Amethysts, Crimsons, and Ambers had sent two candidates apiece. Nine dragons, all eager to be declared the next consort for the Jade Court.

The hopefuls gathered in the middle of the massive ring of dragons, awaiting the start of the trials. From what Belen understood, they would take part in three challenges.

A mighty roar reverberated across the island valley. A magnificent green dragon soared in, alighting near the hopefuls. Gideon, the Jade Prince. Like other creatures, dragons didn't always breed true to a single color, so often an Emperor or Empress might have scales a different shade from that of their court. But the Jade rulers were all green—and Belen hoped that gave her an advantage, as the only green dragoness in contention.

Gideon spread his wings wide and dipped his horns to the assembled hopefuls. He surveyed them with a piercing gaze, noting each one before he spoke. His voice was deep and resonant, carrying over the entire island valley.

"Welcome and fair skies," he said. "You are here today to compete for the honor of being my consort, and I thank you all for participating."

The crowd of dragons roared their approval, Belen included.

"Today we shall begin our first trial," Gideon continued when the clamor died down. "A test of agility—you must weave through a series of obstacles while avoiding any contact with them. The fastest dragon across the finish line will be declared the winner!"

"Where will we do this?" one of the candidates, a dragon with yellow-gold scales, asked.

Gideon gave them a toothy grin. "Follow me and witness the marvels of the drakes of Jadefire Island!"

Drakes? Belen touched a claw to her golden chain, but didn't have time to wonder as Gideon took off. The air was filled with the thunder of wings as audience and hopefuls alike followed the prince.

Gideon led them to a box canyon at the far end of the island. The dragons perched along the rim, peering down. Strange rock formations seemed to have reared up from the ground like spires. As Belen watched, a tiny dragon stood at the entrance to the canyon, scratching at the ground with a claw.

Belen leaned closer to her nearest neighbor, the gold who had spoken up earlier. "What's that dragon doing?"

"Drake. *Softscale drake*," the yellow nearly sneered.

Belen scowled. She couldn't fathom why the yellow dragon spoke in such a way. Wasn't that disrespectful to the Jade Court? "What do you mean?"

"*Magic*," the other dragon clarified, and in the single word, Belen understood.

Her home court didn't have drakes, but she had heard whispers of them. They were smaller and different in a way that made the hardscale dragons vaguely uncomfortable. Empress Malvika had once expressed relief that the Ceruleans boasted no drakes—which had made Belen uneasy about the gifted chain. But the Jade Court *did*...and not only that, flaunted them.

Gideon landed beside the drake, nodding in approval. "Behold the wondrous work of Asher! My potential consorts, you will be called down here one by one and fly through this course. But have a care...it's not as simple as it seems."

Belen's brow furrowed. "What?"

As if in answer, the Jade Prince glanced at the drake. "Asher, please show them the hazards they face."

The drake nodded, stepping forward. Belen squinted, trying to see what he did. As far as she knew, he buried his claws in the dirt...

And the spires came alive.

They flailed like the tentacles of some massive stone kraken, snapping through the air before slamming into the ground. Belen's pulse sped at the sight, and she heard the whimper of another candidate.

"*Impossible*. That's what this is," the yellow dragon growled. "Gideon wants to stay a widower!"

Belen lifted her chin, determination swelling. She was smaller than many of the other contenders, which would be a boon in this situation. "Not impossible. The prince wants the best, and the best he shall have."

The first dragoness fluttered down to the course when Gideon called her name. Belen watched as she flew off like a shot as soon as the time began. But the dragoness was at a disadvantage—as the first, she didn't know what might happen. In only seconds, one of those writhing stone pillars pinned her to the ground.

"This is unfair!" the dragon complained as the drake called off his abomination. "No one can do this."

Gideon studied her with glittering eyes. "No? Well, if everyone fails, then I suppose you'll be on the same footing for the next challenge, which will be of a more *intellectual* nature." He turned away and called for the next competitor.

All the other dragons went through the course, with only one of them succeeding—a red dragon who was dainty compared to the others. Then it was Belen's turn.

She flew down to the course, giving the prince a regal bow. "Thank you for the opportunity, Your Grace. I hope to do you proud."

He tilted his head. The other dragons had said little to him when they came down, too focused on the task at hand. His ear-flaps pricked at her, then Gideon nodded. "And I wish the same. Prepare yourself...and...*begin!*"

Belen took off, her wings beating powerfully. She had watched the other dragons carefully, analyzing their failures. She was determined to not make the same mistakes.

The other dragons looked on in disbelief as Belen zig-zagged past each pillar, barely missing them with a scales-width of space between her body and their jagged edges. She flipped over one spire before dropping down in an arc and gliding across a narrow ledge that ran along one wall of the canyon.

It was almost too easy—she could feel herself getting cocky as she pushed forward even faster, twisting her body around a spire before making a sharp turn to avoid another that flailed at her like a great tentacle.

Finally, Belen emerged from the course unscathed. She rose into the air, flying in a triumphant loop before landing beside the Prince.

The other dragons roared with excitement as Gideon smiled in approval. He motioned for them to stop and said, "That was remarkable! You have all exceeded my expectations—and one of you has done so much more. Belen, you have succeeded with the fastest time. I declare you the winner."

Belen arched her neck and scratched at the turf with a claw, the very image of humility. "It was nothing, Prince Gideon." But inside, she celebrated. *One down, two to go.*

CHAPTER
FIVE

The second challenge began bright and early the next morning. Belen arrived to find the valley from the previous day empty of all but the hopefuls. The royals hadn't invited the audience? She peered skyward and found the Emperor and Empress on a ridge overlooking them, tails twitching.

"Prince Gideon chose yesterday's trial, and now it is my turn," Empress Cordova announced, her voice airy and bright. "Today's task requires you to combine your minds and show off your intellect."

Work together? Belen shifted uneasily. By nature, dragons didn't work together very well. Hardscales were temperamental and conceited, believing they were more than enough for any task. Even Belen knew she fell prey to this.

The other contenders grumbled, no doubt feeling the same. But none of them spoke out against it.

Cordova nodded. "Excellent. We will split you into two teams. Your goal is to solve a series of puzzles. Each puzzle will provide you with the clue to lead you to the next. The first team to complete all four puzzles wins."

After the first test, three dragons were removed, leaving only six. Before long, Belen found herself teamed up with a yellow dragon named Patli and a magenta named Andressa. Neither was excited to work with others, but before long, they gathered in a knot, prepared to do their best.

A copper-scaled drake approached, bearing a scroll. The drake cleared her throat, unrolling it. "Empress Cordova has charged me with assisting you with this task. You'll find the riddles written upon parchment."

Patli bared her fangs. "You think we have sullied ourselves with the human scratching?"

"She does *not*, which is why she is here," Belen said, surprised that the yellow dragon hadn't made that connection. Only a few dragons knew how to read, mostly those who had studied with the Seer at the Vault of Fate. And drakes, it seemed.

Belen edged closer, peering over the drake's shoulder. To her surprise, the ink scratches on the page made sense. "I am a necklace of the ocean, a circle of life that embraces the island. What am I?"

"You can read?" Andressa's eyes widened.

Belen winced. She shouldn't have said that aloud. But she had been so surprised by the revelation... The golden chain shifted against her scales, a reminder. Was the gift responsible? There was no other explanation.

"It's not hard," Belen muttered instead. Because in truth, it hadn't been. The shapes on the page simply made sense to her.

"You're correct about the words," the drake said, sounding pleased. "Now you must decipher the meaning."

"A necklace," Patli repeated, tail twitching with agitation. "Islands don't have necklaces."

"It's a riddle. It's not literal," Belen said. What could it be? The tide? The sea? But as far as answers went, those ideas were too broad.

"The sky, maybe?" Andressa ventured.

Belen shook her head. "That's too big. It needs to be more specific like…" Her brow furrowed. "The lagoon!"

The drake nodded. "Very good. Hurry to the lagoon to find the next riddle."

Belen led the way, her mind still reeling with awe at her newfound ability. The other dragons and drake followed behind as they made their way toward the lagoon.

They approached a small sandy cove that overlooked the turquoise waters of the lagoon, and Belen's eyes widened when she saw what awaited them there: a large boulder with a sheet of parchment tied around it with a black ribbon.

"This must be it!" Belen exclaimed, racing to it with excitement coursing through her veins. She quickly untied the ribbon and unrolled the parchment, revealing a new riddle written in neat black ink.

"I am a home to the vulnerable, a place where many grow, but if you step on me, I'll disappear. What am I?" Belen frowned as she concluded the riddle. Vulnerable? Her brow furrowed as she examined the different bits and failed to make connections.

Patli and Andressa were invigorated by solving the first riddle, and both mulled over a variety of answers, though none of them were suitable. After a few moments, Andressa flexed her claws in the sand. "I've got it! Coral reef. On my home island, we're told to be careful of the reef when we go swimming so we don't kill it."

The drake beamed. "That is correct." She glanced at the lapping waves. "One of you must swim out to the reef and find the clue in a waterproof tube."

"I've got it." Patli slogged into the waves, vanishing beneath the froth before Belen or Andressa volunteered. The yellow dragon return moments later, clutching the tube in her claws, seawater dripping from her scales. She tossed the tube to Belen. "I can't let *you* have all the fun. I'm here to win this, too."

The next riddle led them to a cluster of mangroves, where they picked up the final parchment. "I am always hungry, and I must be fed; but the more I am given, the thinner I get. What am I?" Belen tilted her head, thoughtful.

"Fire," Patli said after a moment. "But I didn't see any signs of a fire anywhere."

"No, but I think I saw the remains of an old bonfire on the beach at the lagoon," Andressa supplied. "When you were swimming to the reef."

"Only one way to find out," Belen said, and together they flew back to the lagoon.

True to the magenta dragon's word, there was an old bonfire on the beach—and not only that, Empress Cordova stood by the ashes, waiting. She smiled at them. "Well, I see there are three of you that can work together without breaking into a brawl! Because of that alone, I would declare you the victors. But you also succeeded at solving every riddle. And for that, you should be proud. Welcome to the final challenge, consort hopefuls."

CHAPTER
SIX

Emperor Danilo greeted them bright and early the next morning. Only Belen, Andressa, and Patli remained in contention. The losers had joined the ranks of the audience, and today it appeared they were permitted to watch the final challenge.

The sun was just beginning to peek out over the horizon as the regal green dragon flew to an overlook and addressed his court. His voice echoed through the crisp morning air as he announced, "Today's challenge will be a test of strength. The three of you shall face off in a three-way battle!" He paused, letting his words sink in before continuing.

Emperor Danilo raised his claws dramatically, gesturing towards the valley. "A platform has been set up for this battle. It is surrounded by a ring of pillars that reach up to the sky. Atop these pillars are flags representing each contender—bright green for Belen, brilliant red for Andressa, and deep gold for Patli. This will be your battlefield; here is where your strength, courage, and wit are put to the ultimate test!" He went on to explain that the winner would be the dragoness who claimed all three flags.

"Emperor, are we allowed to harm one another?" Andressa asked.

The Jade Emperor fixed her with a look. "The life of a royal is not as cosseted as it seems. Use tooth and claw, tail and scale. Use everything you have to win and survive—even if it means killing another."

Belen swallowed, her eyes widening. She had known this might be dangerous...but she hadn't expected this. She took a calming breath, reminding herself she had an advantage the other two lacked. Chandra had seen her as the Jade Empress. And if Chandra truly *was* a Seer, her vision would come true.

"Do you understand?" Danilo asked, tone grave.

All three nodded.

"Excellent. The challenge begins now!"

What? Belen only had time to blink and register the start as Patli and Andressa surged toward the pillars, each with their sights on the other's flag. Belen shook her head, uncertainty growing. They were both larger than she was. Did she even stand a chance?

With dogged determination, Belen pushed off and flew to the pillar that held her own flag, watching as Patli snagged the red flag and Andressa captured the gold. No doubt before long they would come for Belen's. She had to make that a problem for them.

Belen narrowed her eyes. Danilo hadn't said their flags needed to *stay* on the pillars. So, in theory, she could move hers. Belen stripped it from the flagpole, heart thumping as she considered what to do next. Should she carry it around with her? *No, too easy to lose...*

Hide it. She needed to hide it. Belen considered stuffing it into her treasure gullet for safekeeping, but realized that might encourage the larger dragons to rip her apart. No, she had to hide it somewhere else.

Glancing over her wing, she found Patli chasing after Andressa, roaring in fury. Good. They were too distracted to pay attention to her. She pushed off from her pillar, gliding out of the valley and to the mangroves. Belen tied her flag to a shade-dappled root, then returned to the field of battle—

Patli slammed into her, knocking Belen off course. The audience gasped as Belen bounced off the valley wall, the breath torn from her lungs. Everything hurt. The world swirled around Belen's vision as she tried to clear her head. The large yellow dragon stood over her, sides heaving from exertion.

"Where is your flag?" Patli demanded.

"Where's Andressa?" Belen asked, mostly because her brain was still dazed and it was the only thing she could think of.

Patli snarled. "*Where is your flag?*" Her fangs loomed uncomfortably close to Belen's neck.

"It'll be hard to find if you kill me, that's for certain," Belen shot back, earning a frustrated roar.

At that moment, Andressa swooped in from behind and launched a surprise attack on Patli, clawing at her wings and shrieking. Belen felt a surge of hope. If the other two were busy fighting, it would give her time to escape and get the flags. She scrambled out of the way as they fought, locking eyes with Andressa's briefly as she flew by. Was that understanding in her gaze?

Belen didn't have time to consider it further as she quickly noticed two flags fluttering atop Andressa's spire. Gold and red. She soared to the spire, talons outstretched to snag the banners, and shoved off again. The audience cheered wildly as

Belen flew back to the mangroves and moments later returned with all three flags in her claws. As she soared higher and higher into the sky, Belen knew without a doubt that she had won this challenge.

CHAPTER
SEVEN

A day later, Belen stood in a row with Patli and Andressa. They were all alive, but battered. Andressa had a broken wing, though a drake had tended it and now the magenta held it tenderly close to her body. Deep claw marks scored the yellow dragon's haunches and torso.

By comparison, Belen had gotten off lightly. She had bruises from colliding with the valley wall and scratches from Patli, but little more.

Prince Gideon stood in front of his parents. The royal dragons' scales gleamed like sun-fired emeralds in the early morning light.

"I wish to thank all of the contenders for taking part," Gideon announced, his gaze drifting over the remaining hopefuls. "Choosing a consort is not a simple task, and the Jade Court requires the best of the best."

At his words, a low rumble fell over the audience. Belen glanced over her folded wings when she heard the breathy mention of the deceased consort from a spectator. She clenched her jaw, shifting to stare straight ahead.

If the murmurs bothered Gideon, he didn't show it. He ambled up the line of potential consorts, studying each with a critical eye. Finally, he came to a stop before Belen. "I found it odd that the Cerulean Court only sent a single dragoness."

She swallowed. Did she dare reveal that no one else had volunteered? No, that would be an insult, and it wasn't something she could afford. Belen aimed a charming smile at the green prince. "The Cerulean Court only sends the best to such a contest, Prince Gideon."

His nostrils flared. "Indeed. And that is why today, I choose Belen of the Cerulean Court as the Jade Consort."

Belen froze as a chorus of deafening roars rolled over her. It couldn't be true...could it? Chandra's prophecy was under way, with Belen starting down the path of the Jade Empress. She lifted her chin, eyes gleaming with pride. She stepped forward, meeting her new mate's gaze. "And I choose you." She was not a pawn to be used. Belen was determined to be a force in her own right.

Gideon's toothy grin widened, pleased by her response. "I would expect nothing less."

The unsuccessful competitors grumbled and slipped into the anonymity of the dragon audience. Gideon stepped beside Belen, his scales a shade lighter than her own deep emerald. "I present to you, the Jade Consort!" And with that declaration, he leaped into the air, wings spread wide. Belen followed.

The Jade Court erupted into celebration—a feast was prepared that afternoon, and music provided by the drakes drifted through the air. Courtiers came forward to make their introductions, and Belen was pleased to find Sivarth among them. The red dragon winked before bowing low to her.

The Emperor and Empress of the Jade Court made moving speeches about the joys of welcoming a new consort into their family. Gideon, too, gave a rousing speech, even recounting his excitement at watching Belen thread her way through the enchanted rocks of the first challenge. By the end of the evening, Belen felt as if she might float away on the next cloud.

"You've endured many rigors, so we'll delay our mating flight for a day to allow you to recover," Gideon whispered as they left the celebration together. His wing brushed against hers. "I hope you don't mind."

Belen raised her scaled brows. "I could use rest, though I will admit I was looking forward to having you all to myself."

He blinked. "You're rather bold."

"I'm a dragon who knows what I want," Belen corrected. And she knew the path she was on—the one she was determined to change. There would be no heartache, no loss. Only victory, love, and joy.

Gideon nodded. "This is good. My last consort...she was more reserved." He sighed, an edge of sadness in his voice.

Belen was about to ask about the previous consort when a sheen of familiar blue scales illuminated the darkness ahead. She drew up short, staring. "Chandra?"

The Seer sat in the middle of the path, tail wrapped around her body and wings folded. Her gaze was unfocused, though she still seemed to stare at Belen. Chandra nodded slowly, as if she had heard a question that hadn't been asked. "Yes, I have come." Her voice was low and serious. "I beg you not to follow this path. The heartbreak before you is...insurmountable."

Beside her, Gideon bristled. "What is the meaning of this?"

Belen growled, a warning low in her throat. "Do not ruin my moment of happiness, Chandra."

The azure dragoness lowered her head. "I've come to spare you misery."

The prince glanced between the pair. "What is this dragon talking about, Belen?"

"Chandra is my sister," Belen said through clenched teeth.

"But she is unwell. She dreams she sees the future, but she does not."

At the declaration, Chandra's head jerked as if she had been struck. "For many months, I have trained under the wing of the Seer of the Vault of Fate. The visions I see are *not* madness. They are truth."

Gideon shifted nervously, as if he were second-guessing his selection. Belen couldn't have that, not now. "I will not allow a prophecy to dictate my life!" she declared, her voice ringing through the night air. "I have come this far and am determined to see it through. I will not let anyone—not even my own sister—stop me." She grabbed Gideon's claw and stepped forward, turning her back on Chandra. "We must go now," she said firmly. She vowed never to look back.

Belen held back tears as she walked away—tears of anger at Chandra's interference and sorrow for the rift she knew this would create with her sister. But the future was hers to shape—and she would make it better than anything even Chandra's visions could have foretold.

CHAPTER
EIGHT

The days that followed were a flurry of activity and joy for Belen as she adjusted to her new role as the Jade Consort. She accompanied the Jade Prince on his daily duties, impressed by how effortlessly he charmed those around him with his engaging smile and kind words.

She was also surprised by his attentiveness to her throughout their time together. He made it known that she was more than just a shiny ornament in his court and took any opportunity to get to know her better. Conversation with him turned into debates, which blossomed into deeper, more meaningful talks. They revealed their hopes and aspirations, fears, and secrets to one another, connecting over their shared love for their Court and their growing bond with each other.

As she became more comfortable in the Jade Court, Belen took the time to engage with the other dragons who made up the heart of the island. She took every opportunity to listen to their stories and ask questions as she sought to learn more about how their Court worked.

In all of her conversations, Belen couldn't help but notice

the growing discontent among the drakes. The Jade Court considered them servants. It took a few weeks for her to understand the responsibilities of the drakes. They cared for the hatchlings, prepared food for the Court, served as sentries for the island, and used their magic in ways Belen didn't fully grasp.

On the outside, the drakes seemed to be treated well enough. They weren't abused, but there was a simmering resentment that Belen detected just below the surface, written in the tense body language of a few drakes. Still, Belen needed to do something. Unrest of any sort needed to be handled.

"Gideon," she began one afternoon as they lay curled together, basking in the sun. "Do you know why the drakes are unhappy?"

He angled his head, frowning. "Unhappy? What makes you think that?"

Belen paused, blinking. How could she explain it to him, if he hadn't noticed it? "They just...look like they're discontent."

The Jade Prince chuckled. "Why would they feel like that? They're a part of the Jade Court, living on the best island in the Dragon Latitudes. They're safe here. There's enough food for everyone. They have the pleasure of serving us."

"But they're not *happy*," Belen insisted. "I'd like to speak to them and find out why. Shouldn't everyone in the Jade Court be content?"

Gideon's brow furrowed. "They're just drakes. But I suppose if it pleases you, ask them." He edged closer, nuzzling her neck lovingly.

The next morning, Belen made her way to a grove where she knew the drakes congregated before starting their day. As she broke through the leafy ferns, the three drakes who had been lounging around stared at her with terror.

"Consort," one of them blurted, bowing low. His scales gleamed like polished obsidian. "We were…ah, that is…"

Belen lifted a claw in what she hoped was a calming gesture. "No need to explain yourself. I wish to have a conversation, if you'll allow it."

The drakes exchanged hesitant looks, then nodded. A coppery female drake gestured to the ground nearby. "Then make yourself welcome, Consort."

Belen settled beneath the shade of a papaya, glancing at the assembled drakes. "Let's see. If I recall correctly, you are Asher, Ignatius, and Macawi." Asher and Macawi had both taken part in the selection process. Asher had used his power to create the living stone pillars, and Macawi had assisted Belen's team in the riddle hunt.

"Yes," Ignatius said, warily tilting his glossy black head. "Few dragons bother to learn our names, aside from those we serve regularly."

"I'm not most dragons," Belen replied, sitting up straighter. She hoped it made her appear regal and assured. Like she had authority in the Jade Court. She would, one day. "I will speak plainly. I've noticed that the drakes aren't happy."

All three froze. The black drake looked as if he was about to flee for his life. Macawi, the copper drake, swallowed. "We love serving the Jade Court." Her voice trembled with the lie.

Belen snorted. "I was hatched at night, but not last night. This is not a trap. I'm here to help. I'd like to know why you're unhappy, and what I can do about it."

The drakes exchanged startled looks again. Ignatius still seemed ready to bolt. Asher, a drake the color of moonstones, sighed. "What does it matter? Nothing will change."

"With that attitude, perhaps not," Belen agreed, eyes narrowed. "But I didn't come to the Jade Court to sit around and have my scales polished all day. I'm here to make an impact. I can't do that without information."

Asher blinked in surprise. Then he nodded. "If you insist. We're stuck here, Consort. There is no hope for us beyond being servants to dragons our entire lives. We are not even allowed to leave the island."

Belen frowned. "I was informed you don't need to migrate. No treasure gullets."

Macawi nodded. "We don't have treasure gullets to bring back metal and gems, but that doesn't mean we want to stay here forever. There's a big, wide world out there. We'd like to see it."

While Belen didn't understand the attraction to the idea, it was reasonable. "I see. What else?"

"We're left out of all decision making," Ignatius spoke up. "Not a single drake has the ear of the Emperor or Empress."

Belen shot a look at Asher. "I thought you were Gideon's friend."

"Dragons are not friends with drakes," Asher said, voice taut. "I serve him. Gideon is kind, but I am still subservient to him." Something flashed in his eyes. Resentment. And something else...something dangerous.

Belen suppressed a shiver. "Anything else I should know?"

"The larger dragons disrespect us," Macawi said after a moment.

Belen sighed. "The apexes and leviathans disrespect anyone without brute strength to back them, even other dragons." She shook her head. "Nothing new there."

"It's not just the leviathans and apexes." Macawi glanced down at a long scrape on her shoulder that Belen hadn't noticed until then. "Every dragon likes to remind us we're smaller. Weaker."

"I'm sorry for that," Belen said, meaning every word. "I'll

admit, you've given me a lot to think about. I'll take it back to Prince Gideon and discuss the matter. I'm hopeful we'll find a way to change your circumstances."

They gave her dubious looks. "Best of luck, Consort," Ignatius said.

"I don't need luck," Belen said, rising. She was going to forge her own destiny, starting with this topic.

She found Gideon resting on the beach, delicately plucking grapes one after the other and popping them into his mouth. A drake stood sentry nearby. Belen glanced at the drake, then settled down beside her mate.

"Did you have a pleasant chat?" Gideon asked.

Belen nodded, steeling herself. "I did. And I discovered we must address the grievances of the drakes. They feel undervalued. We should work towards creating a more inclusive Court."

Gideon offered her a grape. "I understand your concerns, and your heart is in the right place. However, we cannot change the circumstances of the drakes. Things are as they are for a reason, and the dragons of our Court would not tolerate the drakes being free or having more influence. We must maintain the balance of power to ensure the stability of the Jade Court."

Belen frowned, her heart heavy with disappointment. But this was a minor setback. She would bide her time. One day she would be the Jade Empress.

One day, she would be the change.

CHAPTER NINE

The Jade Court was a swirling vortex of politics and social maneuvering, and Belen threw herself into its depths with reckless curiosity. Meetings were battlegrounds, hidden behind a veneer of pleasantries. Feasts were not just about food; they were about alliances, visible and invisible.

Early on, she identified the players who would be her allies and those who would be obstacles. Tarnis, a dragon with scales as black as his ambitions, was one to watch out for. She'd caught him glaring at her more than once, his eyes like cold embers.

But it was Councilor Miralda who caught her attention the most. The elder dragon's scales were a living work of art, shimmering in hues that mimicked the sky at dusk. "Councilor, I need your guidance," she finally mustered the courage to say, approaching the wise dragon during a feast celebrating the Emperor's hatching day.

Miralda's eyes softened, and she led Belen to a quiet alcove. As they basked in the dying rays of the sun, Miralda unraveled the intricacies of Jade Court politics. "You have to understand, every dragon here has an agenda, a goal they fiercely guard," she confided. Belen listened, her mind racing to keep up, absorbing the invaluable wisdom like a sea sponge.

Belen's influence didn't just grow—it erupted like a volcano, reshaping the landscape of the Jade Court. As the newly appointed emissary, she was the face and voice during diplomatic missions to other islands. Her ability to connect with others was almost magical, turning skeptics into believers.

One of her most memorable encounters was with Regent Veyra of the Crimson Court, a dragon known for her ruthlessness in negotiations. They met in a dimly lit chamber, the air thick with tension.

"Your demands are a bit... excessive, don't you think?" Belen said, studying a parchment that outlined Veyra's terms.

Veyra leaned in, her eyes narrowing. "I find them reasonable."

"Reasonable for the Crimson Court, perhaps, but what about for the Jade Court, not to mention the others?" Belen asked, tapping the paper with a talon.

"The well-being of other courts is not my concern, Jade Consort. My loyalty is to the Crimson Court. What makes you think you can advocate for everyone?" Veyra retorted.

Belen looked Veyra squarely in the eyes. "Because when one court suffers, we all suffer, Regent Veyra. We're bound together, whether we like it or not. It's time we start acting like it."

After a long pause, Veyra finally spoke, her tone softer. "Jade Consort, you are full of surprises."

Belen nodded. "Strength lies in unity, Regent Veyra. Isolation only weakens us."

Veyra chuckled, her eyes flashing with what could only be described as respect. "You're unlike any dragon I've ever met."

"And that, Regent, is exactly what I strive to be," Belen declared, a triumphant smile crossing her face.

Soon, whispers of her diplomatic feats spread across the courts, converting even the staunchest naysayers. Belen had become more than just a voice; she was a force, steering not just the destiny of the Jade Court but shaping the entire dragon world.

Yet she never lost sight of her goals. She challenged the prophecy that haunted her, advocating for the drakes in the shadows of the Court.

Walking the beach with Gideon one evening, she raised the subject once more. "Gideon, I know you said we couldn't change the drakes' circumstances, but I can't help but feel we must do something. They deserve a better life."

Gideon sighed, his gaze drawn to the moonlit waves. "I understand your compassion for them, but you must remember the delicate balance of power within our Court. We cannot simply change such things without consequences."

Her determination flared. "I know, but we can find a way. I believe we can make the Jade Court a better place for all its members, including the drakes."

Gideon marveled at her relentless passion. He nuzzled her affectionately. "You're a force to be reckoned with, my love. If anyone can make a difference, it's you."

CHAPTER TEN

Asher

"Come. We must speak." Ignatius bumped his hip against Asher, interrupting the Stoneshaper drake.

"I was in the middle of something," Asher murmured, his claws rasping against a smooth stone orb. His friend knew he hated interruptions when he was at work, yet Ignatius persisted.

"It will wait, my love," Macawi's soft voice piped up as she approached. Her eyes glowed in the evening moonlight. "I know you're distracting yourself from your true feelings by burying yourself in work."

Was he that obvious? Perhaps to his mate, who knew him better than anyone else. He was helpless to live out his internal dreams of destroying the dragons, one by one. They'd had a difficult enough time removing the previous Consort, and she had simply been their test.

Asher, Macawi, and Ignatius found a secluded grove, far from the prying eyes of the dragons, where they could discuss their situation. The discontent among the drakes had grown stronger since their conversation with Belen, and they knew they couldn't rely on her to solve their problems.

"She wears a nexus chain," Asher murmured once they settled in the grove. He lifted a claw to pull out the golden chain that encircled his neck, usually hidden beneath his flexible scales. "I know you saw that, Macawi. How did Belen get a nexus chain?" His gaze snapped to Ignatius.

The black drake's lips peeled back as if he were about to fight off a hidden accusation. "Don't look at me! I may craft magical items, but I'm surely not the only one with the talent." Ignatius snorted out a breath.

"She *arrived* with it," Macawi said, slinging a wing over Asher's back and drawing him closer. He liked that, and he settled against his mate's warm side. "And then she *won*. Do you think perhaps she was sent to liberate us?"

Oh, at times his darling mate was far too optimistic. Asher shook his head. "What, you think the drakes of the Forgotten Library would send a *dragon* to free us?"

Macawi aimed a wounded look at him. "It's possible not all dragons intend to keep us as servants. I think she really *does* want to help us."

"Perhaps she does," Ignatius said with a prim nod. "But from what I see of the Court, she will have an impossible time convincing the others."

"Or if she does, it will take *years*." Asher shook his head. "And we've already waited long enough." He had reached the point where he was unwilling to wait any longer. Macawi had laid her first clutch of eggs last week—a veritable miracle, after many years of trying. Asher didn't want his children born into servitude. Not when there was so much more out in the world for them.

Macawi rested her head against his shoulder, as if she

sensed his thoughts. "But what can we do? The dragons are too powerful. We don't stand a chance against them."

Ignatius lifted a hand and stroked his claws over his own nexus chain, a nervous habit. "Maybe we don't need to fight them directly. What if we sought allies outside of the Jade Court?"

Asher frowned. "What do you mean? It's unlikely any of the other Courts would move against the Jades. They're all *dragons*." He had pondered the idea of luring another Court in to conquer the Jades. Maneuvering some sort of territorial dispute. But it had seemed like nothing more than swapping out one master for another.

Ignatius looked thoughtful. "There's a world beyond the Jade Court. And it's filled with humans who might be willing to help us."

Macawi tilted her head, intrigued. "Humans? How could they help us?"

"Well," Ignatius said, "we have unique abilities, and humans are fascinated by magic. Perhaps we could form an alliance with them, using our powers to our mutual advantage."

Asher considered the idea. As far as plans went, it wasn't terrible. Ignatius was right. Humans would be interested in his ability to bring stone to life. It would be useful for construction or protection. Macawi was gifted with plants, able to manipulate vegetation in a variety of ways. And Ignatius was skilled at crafting jewelry that held magic—especially the nexus chains that helped the drakes focus their powers.

Macawi made a soft sound of consideration. "If we were to approach the humans, we'd need to do so in a way they wouldn't find threatening. We can't reveal our true selves to them right away." They had all heard tales of encounters between dragons and humans. Dragons usually had the advantage—and though drakes *looked* like dragons, a human would have a much easier time killing one.

"And that is why I suggested humans," Ignatius whispered, gesturing between them. "We can assume their form. It would be the perfect way to approach them and gain their trust."

The tip of Asher's tail twitched. Ignatius was right. Every drake could shapeshift, but most could only master one other form. As whelps, they chose a shape and, in secret, practiced the change until it became second nature. The drakes of the Jade Court could shift into humans, pegasi, unicorns, griffins, elves, Theilians, and Knossans.

"Well, this is certainly not the *worst* idea," Asher agreed, warming up to it. "But it will take time." He exchanged a worried look with Macawi, who leaned into him in a show of comfort.

Ignatius nodded. "Exactly. We'll have to be delicate about this. We need to find the right humans to ally with."

Macawi glanced around, making sure they were still alone. "If we're going to do this, we *must* be cautious. If the dragons uncover our plans..." She swallowed. Macawi didn't need to say more. They knew the price for discovery was death.

"I'll do the initial survey," Ignatius volunteered. "With my speciality, the dragons understand I must leave on occasion in search of materials."

In fact, of all the drakes belonging to the Jade Court, Ignatius was the most traveled. He had been to many of the islands in the Dragon Latitudes to barter for items he needed for his craft. The drake had learned to fit in reasonably well with humans, and in turn had advised Asher and Macawi on all things human.

"And perhaps in your travels you can uncover the location of the Forgotten Library," Macawi suggested, her eyes glimmering with hope.

The Forgotten Library is a myth. But Asher dared not say it aloud—he didn't relish an argument with his beloved. If there was an island teeming with other drakes out there, why didn't any of them know about it?

There were other drakes in the Dragon Latitudes, that much was certain. But like Asher, they were subjects of their dragon courts. The Pearls and Ambers had the only other notable populations of drakes, though they weren't in the same sort of subservient position as the Jade drakes, from what Asher had learned.

"I will certainly try," Ignatius agreed, tone solemn. He glanced at Asher. "Our tomes of magic had to come from *somewhere*, my friend."

Asher raised a scaly brow. "Yes. Our *ancestors* wrote them."

In the drake warrens, a collection of special books of magic remained hidden from dragon eyes. Some of the books theorized on the origins of drake magic. Others attempted to explain it it, offering simple lessons to help young drakes learn to harness their abilities. They were a precious collection, and Asher was determined to escape the island with them, too.

Ignatius sighed, rolling his eyes. They'd had this quarrel before. The black drake shrugged. "So, it's decided, then? I'll begin scouting?"

Asher and Macawi exchanged a look, and then both nodded. "We deserve this. Our *children* deserve this," Macawi whispered.

CHAPTER
ELEVEN

True to his word, Ignatius searched for allies. To Asher's great surprise, it didn't take him long to find a likely match. Before he knew it, he and Macawi were devising a way to bundle up their eggs for travel.

With the help of a few other drakes who they brought in on the plan, they created slings to hold the eggs and the books Asher wanted to keep from the dragons. Then he, Macawi, and Ignatius set off into a starless night, winging toward what Asher hoped was a brighter future.

After a perilous journey through late-season storms, they arrived at the island. Dead Man's Dare, so Ignatius said the island was named, was far prettier than the moniker implied. Thick jungles appeared to take up most of the land, though that had worked in the human's favor. Asher noted a plume of smoke in the distance, a sure sign of habitation.

Macawi shivered in anticipation, her scales chiming softly. "We made it. I can't believe we made it."

Ignatius chuckled. "Find a hiding place for your little ones. I'll go wander into town and find my...friend."

Asher watched the black drake hurry off, then helped his mate as she hunted for the perfect location for the eggs.

"I'm so relieved," Macawi whispered as she dug a depression between a pair of mango trees. She nestled the eggs into the hole, then laid her claws against the bark of the nearest tree.

"It only gets better from here." Asher smiled as he watched his mate work.

The roots of the mango tree writhed like sleepy snakes, then slipped over the eggs in a tight, protective netting. Macawi found a nearby thorny vine, encouraging it to come closer. She pushed her magic against it, accelerating the vine's growth. Huge thorns burst from the vine as it curled around the eggs.

"There," she said, settling onto her haunches with satisfaction. "My plants will be the perfect caretakers until we return," Macawi crooned to the eggs. "We'll be back soon, my loves."

With their eggs protected, Asher and Macawi hurried to catch up with Ignatius. When the first signs of humanity became visible, both drakes assumed their human forms.

It had taken time to figure out the nuances of these forms. Humans, they discovered, had a tendency to parade around in finery they called clothing. Asher assumed it was because their hides were too thin and they had little in the way of hair or scales to offer protection. This was the one downside to choosing the human form. Though, Asher recalled, elves were the same way.

"How do I look?" Macawi smiled at him, her short reddish-brown hair bobbing around her slender shoulders as she spun in a blue dress that hugged her body like a second skin.

"Not bad," Asher said, distracted by his own change. Somehow, he'd shifted with a pair of trousers and sandals, but no shirt. *Stupid human clothes. So confusing.*

Macawi rammed an elbow into his side.

Asher gasped, aiming a look at her. "What was that for?"

"Drake or human, *never* tell a female *not bad*." She lifted her chin, eyes narrowed.

Asher blinked, then laughed. "I'm sorry. I was trying to figure out what happened to my shirt."

"You don't see *me* complaining." Macawi grinned at him. "The human form isn't as attractive as a drake, but as far as they go…I would say you're *not bad*."

Asher raised his brows. "And now you're teasing me."

"Maybe." Macawi started forward, hips swaying with each stride. "Keep up, scaleheart."

Asher jogged until he was beside her, and together they made their way to the outskirts of town, where they waited in the deep shadows of a mahogany tree until Ignatius appeared.

The drake wasn't alone. An older, dark-skinned man with a face lined by wrinkles accompanied him. Though the hair crowning his head was grey, there was a sense of power and authority to him. He clutched a book under one arm.

"A wizard," Asher whispered, eyes widening. This was either very good…or very bad. Should he send Macawi away? One of them needed to survive, or the eggs would die…

"We have a friend," Ignatius announced, his voice carrying.

Asher and Macawi exchanged glances, then stepped out of their hiding place. The wizard's gaze landed on them, and Asher felt a shiver course through his body. There was something unsettling about the way the man looked at them, as if he could see through their human forms and into their very souls. Ignatius seemed unfazed, however, and gestured for them to come closer.

"Jeriel, this is Asher and Macawi," Ignatius said, indicating each of them. "More of the drakes I told you about. My dearest friends."

Jeriel's eyes flicked over them once more before settling on Ignatius. "Drakes. And here I thought your kind was lost to myth."

Myth. Like the Forgotten Library. Asher swallowed, not liking this. And he didn't care for the fact that Ignatius had already told this human what they were. But they had to show a united front, so he didn't call out his friend.

"We're very much alive and well," Asher said instead, eyes narrowed.

The wizard chuckled. "So I see. It's...amazing. That's all."

"Jeriel came to the Dragon Latitudes to study dragons," Ignatius supplied.

Jeriel nodded. "I did. I'm from Ravance...don't know if you know where that is. Far, far away."

Asher didn't know, and honestly didn't care. What mattered was that his man had magic and he might help them with their cause. "Ignatius has explained our purpose to you?"

A strange expression crossed Jeriel's face. "Yes. I have mixed feelings on dragons. They're so..." He paused, wonder gleaming in his eyes. "Regal. Beautiful. I could watch them fly all day. But they're also terrible and cruel. I saw one land on a fishing boat a few months ago and eat the crew."

Can't fault them for that. Humans are small and prey-shaped. Asher might have done the same. He might be the same size as Jeriel at the moment, but in his natural form he would tower over the man.

"He says he will help us," Ignatius said.

Jeriel shook his head. "I said I would take your request before the Council when you came back. But I think they'll be receptive, given how many we've lost to dragons over the years."

Macawi lifted her chin. "We have magic. Like you."

The wizard tilted his head. "And unlike me. Yes, Ignatius

told me. I'm the only magic-wielder here, so your presence will be welcomed by some." He cleared his throat. "Ignatius also promised that I could read the books you brought."

Asher bit back a growl. That blasted drake. He glared at Ignatius.

For his part, Ignatius shrugged. "It's a worthwhile trade. He's going to *read* them, not keep them."

From what Asher knew of wizards, most of their spellwork was done via their grimoires. He wasn't worried about the wizard keeping the book, no. Asher was more concerned about the wizard potentially adding drake-specific information to his own grimoire.

I might have to kill this wizard when all this is said and done, Asher thought with resignation. *But first we have to get that far.*

Jeriel gestured toward the town. "I've been a rude host. Let's not keep talking out here. You're surely tired from your travels. I'll welcome you to my hearth. And tomorrow you can make your plea."

Macawi bit her lower lip. "Are all welcome?"

The wizard turned to her. "What do you mean?"

The female drake put her hands on her hips. "Eggs. I have hidden eggs on the island, and while they're safe for now…"

Jeriel smiled with understanding. "You would feel better if they were near. Yes, of course. They're innocent babes. Worthy of protection. Fetch your eggs and bring them back. Like you, they are welcome here."

Macawi's breath caught and she grabbed Asher's hand, squeezing it in excitement. "I'll be right back!" And then, perhaps forgetting herself, she shifted into her sleek drake form and vaulted into the air.

Jeriel stared, his mouth tipping open. "She just…"

Asher glared at him, ready to defend his mate if needed. "You named us as drakes. That's what we are."

The wizard swallowed, shaking his head as if he were shedding water. "Yes, but there's a difference in *thinking* something is true and seeing it in person." Then he whistled. "Never in all my years did I expect to witness something like that!"

Asher relaxed. The human sounded pleased, which was good. No need to call up an army of stone golems to destroy him...yet. They waited on Macawi's return, and Asher thought that maybe, just maybe, they had a chance.

CHAPTER
TWELVE

"The dragons have command of the sky," Rance, the man Asher presumed to be the leader of the island council, pointed out. He shifted in his seat, nervous in the presence of the drakes.

Some of the humans were reluctant to help. Asher understood—many of them had children, and though his were still in the shell, his heart broke at the thought of them in peril.

Still, they couldn't let fear stop them. Not now. "But so do humans," Asher said

Rance scowled. "We have no griffins or pegasi in the Dragon Latitudes."

"Airships," Macawi piped up. She, Asher, and Ignatius had discussed this part in detail. "You have airships. We saw them in your landing field."

Tori, a dark-haired human female, shook her head. "Airships are too delicate to go against a dragon. One talon scratches the balloon, and every person on that vessel is doomed."

Asher eyed the wizard. "And you have not used magic to fortify it?"

Jeriel frowned. "I'm a wizard. I'm limited to casting the spells I know, and I don't have any like that. You'd need a specialized mage."

"Or a drake," Ignatius said softly, eyes gleaming as he lifted his chin. "I work with metal...I might be able to work with your airship."

"Work with it how?" Rance asked, voice tense.

"Make it capable of standing against a dragon, for one," Ignatius said. He paused. "And even if I can't, there is knowledge in the books—"

"No," Asher growled, whirling on Ignatius. That was a step too far. Let the wizard read the books for himself and discover it, yes. But openly speak of the capabilities of drakes, in public? Absolutely not.

"I doubt it can be done, at any rate," Tori said with a shake of her head. "Even if the balloon is protected, there's a hundred other ways a dragon can take down one of our airships."

"It *can* be done," Ignatius insisted, clearly not caring about Asher's concerns. "Of that, I can promise you." His eyes glittered with determination.

Asher clenched his fists, wishing for his drake form so that he could roar out his frustration. But that wouldn't do. Ignatius had committed them to the course, so what else could he do but go along?

"We can teach you how to fight the dragons," Asher volunteered. He and Macawi had already discussed options. Humans used harpoons to hunt seals and tuna. With the right force behind them, it might be possible to pierce the armor of a hardscale dragon...

Rance traded a look with Jeriel. "You would teach us how to slay your own kind?" Rance asked.

Asher lifted his chin. "We're not *dragons*." In his mind, it was crucial they understand the difference. He didn't want to be linked to their enemies in any way. And the less humans thought drakes and dragons were alike, the better for drakes in the long term.

Jeriel rubbed his palms together. "I think at this point, it's in our best interest to learn what we can."

With the humans convinced, the drakes spent the next several months sharing their knowledge of the dragons. Ignatius went to work with a dozen other humans, including Tori, who seemed to know quite a bit about the airship. They worked to fortify the *Revenant* and make the airship proof against the attack of a dragon.

Asher set to work as well, creating an army of stone constructs that would fight on their side against the Jade Court.

And most surprisingly, week after week, more drakes joined them in the settlement. Many of them prepared to fight the dragons, while others, savoring their first taste of freedom, set off on their own adventures.

Before long, Asher counted fifty drakes who had deserted the Court. Twenty of them stayed, eager to fight the dragons and free the rest of their friends and family who remained on Jadefire Island.

The night before their planned attacked, Asher joined Macawi in their borrowed quarters. Jeriel had set them up in something called a boarding house. The room was small, which meant they were stuck in human form unless they wished to find somewhere to sleep outside.

But their eggs were in the room, and Macawi wouldn't leave them. She had nestled them in the middle of the bed, swaddled in blankets. Macawi lay curled around them, her auburn hair fanned out on the pillow.

"You should stay here," Asher said, not for the first time, as he sat on the edge of the thin mattress.

Her dark eyes locked on his, and she swallowed. He saw the conflict on her face. Macawi reached out and snared his hand with her own. "I'll stay because I must...because *they* need me. But know that my heart flies with you."

Asher leaned down, pressing his forehead against hers. "I'll be back. I promise."

"Don't make promises you can't keep," his mate said, drawing back.

"I fully intend to keep this one," Asher said, resolute. He trailed his soft human fingertips over the rough eggshells. They were warm, and he fancied he could hear the strong heartbeat of the whelps within. "I need to come back for them. For you."

Macawi pressed her lips together. "You say that, and yet continue to go forth with your latest plan."

Asher crossed his arms, giving her a cutting look. "You've been around the Jade Court dragons. The only way they'll understand our message is by making it clear that if they cross us, they will suffer."

"You're going to slay the youngest of them. The ones who have done us no wrong," Macawi shot back, her voice soft.

Asher shook his head. The way he saw it, this was the only way their plan could possibly work. Most of the adult dragons were out on migration, though a few would have returned by now. The Court would be weak, with the strongest and fiercest dragons away.

"If we wait and have a *fair* fight it will be our end," Asher snapped. "There is no such thing as a fair fight with an entire island of dragons!"

Macawi's gaze lingered on their eggs. "And how will we explain this to them when they're old enough to understand?

That their sire had no qualms with slaughtering dragon whelps?"

Asher's lips pulled back into a snarl. "They'll understand that their sire would do anything–*anything*–to give them a chance for freedom. For safety!" His shoulders slumped, and he ran a hand through his short, silvery hair. "By the winds, Macawi. You know I'm not doing this to be cruel. I'm doing this to *survive*."

She nodded, but the uncertainty in her eyes spoke volumes. Macawi didn't argue her point any further, and they both attempted to sleep, though Asher was too nervous of the battle to come.

The day of the attack dawned sunny and warm. Asher had already loaded his golems into the hold of the airship the day before. He watched as the human warriors boarded. He didn't understand all the intricacies of the airship–he'd left that to Ignatius. The other drake stood on the deck in human form, going over plans with the ship's captain, Tori.

Asher stood on the beach with Macawi. She was still a woman, but he was back in his native form. She peered up at him, resting her palm against his chest. Asher hoped she might say something, but she was lost in her thoughts. She let her long human arms encircle his neck in a hug before stepping away to allow him room to take off.

"I promise to return," he whispered to her. But he didn't know if she heard, over the rumble of the airship's engine. Swallowing a lump in his throat, he shook his head. He had to set his sentiments aside. It was time for battle.

He pivoted, spreading his wings to take to the skies.

The flight back to Jadefire Island felt like the calm before the storm. Jeriel's magic cloaked their airship, the *Revenant*, in a veil of clouds, masking their approach. Ignatius stayed aboard, his eyes like steel, as he worked his magic to bolster the airship. Asher was in the sky, joined by an elite team of drakes, their eyes ablaze with a mix of anticipation and dread.

The Revenant hovered, hidden by the clouds, as it crossed over the valley walls. Asher's heart pounded as he scanned below, knowing that the next few moments would set the tone for the battle to come. As they dropped to a lower altitude, Jeriel dispelled the cloud cover, and the airship slid into its battle position.

The first roar of warning met them. Asher spotted the dragon sentry, her scales shimmering like molten lava. "Attack now!" he commanded.

In the realm of aerial combat, drakes were the swift daggers to the dragons' slow-moving swords. Asher led his team in a lightning-fast attack, and within seconds, they overwhelmed the dragon sentry. Her wings were reduced to tatters, and gravity took over, pulling her into a deadly descent from which she would not recover.

As if summoned by an invisible signal, dragons erupted into the valley like a living volcano. Many were youngsters, their wings still too delicate for the rigors of long flights. They were joined by drakes who looked bewildered, their eyes wide as they took in their attacking kin.

The air quivered as a furious roar ripped through the valley. "Betrayers! Traitors on our island!" It was the Emperor, bursting onto the scene with wings unfurled like the sails of a warship. "Destroy them all!"

Asher grinned, flying up to the *Revenant*. This was the moment he had been waiting for. He hailed one of the humans. "Open the doors to the hold."

It was time to fight.

CHAPTER
THIRTEEN

Belen

"And then I said he was—" the drake who had been busily grooming the scales along the crest of Belen's neck froze. The pair were on the beach, beside the nursery bower Belen had dug in the sand and then covered with woven grasses to trap the sun's warmth. "Did you hear something?"

Belen blinked, her eyes opening slowly. Constructing the bower and then laying her clutch of eggs had sapped her energy. It was bliss to simply rest. "I might have heard a roar," Belen murmured, though that was hardly unusual.

"As did I," the drake, Aitana, agreed. "But something about it has me uneasy. Stay here, Consort. I will—"

In a burst of wings, Gideon broke through the nearest vegetation, landing nearby in a great gust of sand. "The Court is under attack!" His sides heaved, as if he had flown as quickly as he could. Gideon's gaze shifted to the bower, and for a beat, pride gleamed in his eyes. "Protect our eggs, Belen."

"Under attack?" Belen repeated, the words sounding strange on her tongue. How was such a thing possible?

The Jade Prince didn't reply. He likely hadn't even heard. He was already away, wings cracking open as he rushed to join the fray.

"They did it. They really did it," Aitana whispered. "It must be."

Belen whirled to stare at her. "Who? What is it?"

The drake's eyes widened, and she took a hesitant step backward. "It's nothing. Perhaps I should go help in the defense."

Before she could skitter away, Belen grabbed the drake's tail. Any other time, she would not have used her size against Aitana, but danger was near and Belen was desperate for answers. She pinned the drake to the ground. *Tell me.*

Aitana squeezed her eyes shut. "Drakes. There were rumors..."

The drakes. Belen gritted her teeth. Over the past several months, drakes had gone missing, never to be seen again. Deserters, Gideon had said. Ungrateful creatures. But he hadn't been bothered by the losses, since there were still more than enough drakes to handle the necessary tasks.

"What do you know?" Belen hissed.

Aitana shook her head. "Nothing. Only rumors, but none of them helpful."

Belen growled. *Traitors.* The drakes were traitors, after all she had tried to do for them! She huffed out a hot, frustrated breath, torn between shielding her beloved eggs, the future of the Jade Court, and going out to protect the young dragons.

She knew one thing she *could* do, though.

"I do not abide treachery," Belen whispered.

Aitana writhed beneath her. "Please!"

Belen sank her talons into the drake. Like the others of her kind, Aitana had soft scales, so piercing them was as easy as slicing a mango. Aitana squealed, struggling as Belen carved a gruesome line from breastbone to abdomen.

"*We trusted you,*" Belen growled, shoving away from the dying drake. She cast a conflicted look at her eggs. Stay with them? She might only delay her own death. Better to face their attackers head on and do what she could against them. Aitana would only be the first to die beneath her claws, she vowed.

Belen rushed from her beachside bower and into the chaos. The screams of dragons and the clashing of metal echoed through the air. Belen's breath caught as she saw drakes battling the dragons of the Jade Court. She rushed towards them, her wings beating fiercely against the wind. Belen let out a deafening roar, causing the drakes to pause in their attacks.

"Traitors!" Belen spat, her eyes blazing with fury. "You turn against your own for what? Power? Greed?"

A drake the color of white marble winged down to her level. "You know it's nothing of the sort, Consort!"

She recognized him. *Asher.* Belen had spoken with him months ago. And now he was a traitor. She narrowed her eyes, tail lashing. "If you had only been patient!"

"We're done waiting around for a freedom you'll never grant. We're here to take it," Asher shot back, gesturing with his claws.

A massive stone fist reared up, wrapping around Belen and snatching her from the sky. She yelped as the fist slammed her into the ground. The world spun in her vision, her head pounding, as the hand released her and rejoined the battle.

Belen pushed up, tottering on her feet. Something in her side hurt. Maybe a cracked rib. Whatever it was, it was a problem for later.

For now, the drakes had to die.

Above the frenzied combat, an enormous airship loomed

like a predator, its harpoons snaking out to strike at any dragon that strayed too near. Belen watched it, her mind whirring. She knew airships had their weak points, and she was ready to exploit them. But first, she needed to rally her forces.

"Jade Court! Group up," she commanded, her voice resonating like a clarion call over the tumult of battle. "You are stronger together." That was a simple tactic her brethren forgot all too often. "Guard our young!" she yelled, knowing that the instinct to protect might just be the glue that held them together.

As if her words had been a spell, the older dragons swooped in, their bodies forming a bulwark around the younger and more vulnerable members of their court. They pushed back against the waves of attacking drakes and human invaders. With a nod of approval, Belen spread her wings wide and soared, her sights set on the menacing airship above.

Belen opted for a roundabout approach, initially flying in the opposite direction of the battle before spiraling upward. She was no novice; a direct attack on the airship would be a fool's errand, making her an easy target for their harpoons.

She dove, talons bared and aimed at the delicate exterior of the balloon. But the moment she struck, it was as if she had hit an invisible wall. A shockwave of pain reverberated through her bones, exacerbating her earlier injury. She let out a sharp gasp as she shoved up and winged away to reassess her strategy.

With a growl of frustration, she muttered, "Magic." The realization hit her like a bolt of lightning. Those winds-forsaken drakes had made a pact with the humans, adding a magical defense she hadn't counted on. It was a betrayal that shattered her expectations, and it fueled her with a renewed, fiery determination.

She went into a dive so quickly the humans manning the harpoons didn't have a chance to get her in their sights. Belen discovered that her dragons had, in fact, pushed the drakes back. Some of the drakes, severely injured, were winging up to the airship, blood spattering the sky in their wake.

Belen came to the ground with the Jade defenders, roaring her defiance as the airship retreated from the scene.

Breathing hard, Belen turned to survey the devastation. The scaled corpses of drake and dragon alike littered the valley. Her heart raced so quickly Belen feared she might collapse. She struggled to master herself, shaking her head as she fought back the terror that replaced her earlier rage.

"Empress," a wounded dragon hissed, bowing to her. "What would you have us do?"

"Empress?" Belen repeated, the word a puzzle. She glanced over her shoulder, searching for Empress Cordova. But the royal emerald dragoness was nowhere to be seen. Which meant… "Are you addressing me?"

"Yes, Empress," the dragon rasped. "Empress Cordova and Emperor Danilo were the first to be slain by the drakes."

The blood froze in Belen's veins. Her legs trembled so badly she almost fell. "I see. First, we should gather the survivors. Take care of the wounded. Set a watch." She paused. "Where is Prince Gideon? Surely he'll have more ideas." This was hard. Belen couldn't do this alone. She could barely stand! Her mate would help, of this she was certain.

Councilor Miralda limped up. "Empress, perhaps you should walk with me."

Belen nodded, moving alongside the orange dragon. Miralda was silent as they slowly strode east, weaving around the gutted corpses of drakes and the smashed bodies of dragons. Rubble from a stone golem partially buried a dragon with brilliant green scales…

"No!" Belen wailed as Miralda led her to the front of the dragon. Gideon, his eyes closed, as if he were sleeping.

Belen swooped over to him, her eyes blurred with tears, and shoved a heavy chunk of stone off his wing. His body lay limp, unresponsive. Fighting back a sob that clawed at her throat, she placed her trembling claws gently against the smooth scales of his neck. The chilling absence of warmth hit her like a dagger to the heart.

"Wake up," she whimpered, her voice tinged with desperation. "Gideon, my love. Wake up. Wake up, wake up!" Each repetition was a shard of her shattered heart, each syllable an echo of her soul's cry. She threw back her head and unleashed a guttural roar of agony that seemed to shake the sky. "Wake up! *Wake up!*"

"Empress..." Miralda whispered close to her ear-flap.

"Wake up!" Belen screamed, her words echoing off the valley walls.

Gideon still didn't move.

Belen slumped beside him, vaguely aware of Miralda slinking away to leave her to mourn in privacy. *This.* This was what Chandra had warned her of, so long ago. She was the Jade Empress, but at the great cost of everyone she loved. Of much of the young of her Court. And she had been so certain she could escape the claws of fate.

She would do something about the prophecy later. For the moment, she allowed her heart to shatter into a thousand tiny pieces.

CHAPTER
FOURTEEN

Belen surveyed the ruins of the Jade Court before her, wings folded protectively close like a sort of armor. It had been two long weeks since the attack, and the migrating dragons had returned to find their world forever changed.

"Empress." Miralda's voice was soft, almost reverential, as she hobbled beside Belen. They were walking toward the nursery bower, a place that once symbolized hope and now stood in shambles. "What are your orders?"

Belen felt the weight of the world on her scales. In the sanctuary of her deepest feelings, she wanted to retreat into solitude, to wrestle with the gaping hole that Gideon's loss had left. But that was a luxury she couldn't afford. She was the Jade Empress. The eggs, the future of her lineage and Gideon's, were depending on her.

After a thoughtful silence, Belen found her voice, its timbre laced with resilience. "We rebuild."

Miralda's eyes met hers, then lowered. "Empress, without the drakes, who will do the work?"

Anger surged within Belen at the mention of drakes.

"We've seen the treachery of drakes. We don't need them. We will build a new Jade Court—by dragons, for dragons."

Miralda winced, her scales shimmering in the sunlight. "Our kind is not accustomed to such menial tasks."

Belen stopped, her eyes narrowing. She hadn't considered that, and it was a fair point. Maybe they did need help, at least until they learned to fend for themselves.

"Choose a representative to send to the nearest Courts. Cerulean for certain, and perhaps Amethyst. Request aid for our rebuilding efforts."

Miralda raised her scaly brow. "Won't this be an admission of weakness?"

Weakness. Miralda had a point—to show weakness now opened them to attack from another dragon court. But at the moment Belen didn't care. Based on what Chandra had told her, she didn't think it would come to that. "Send the representative. We're not in a position to rebuild alone." Belen glanced at her nest. "And Miralda? I'll require our most trustworthy apex dragon to watch my eggs for a week."

"A week?" the Councilor blurted. "Where will you be?"

"There is someone I must visit."

Belen said no more on the topic as she made her preparations for travel. Miralda, ever the efficient Councilor, promptly found a suitable apex dragon to watch over Belen's unhatched eggs. With that settled, she launched herself into the sky, her wings heavy with more than just the physical exertion.

She flew over the Sanguine Sea, the waves below reflecting her own turbulent emotions—grief, anger, a sense of loss so profound it was palpable. As she flew, the Vault of Fate began to take shape in the distance. It looked like any other island in the Dragon Latitudes, but its very essence pulsed with an ancient power emanating from the temple at its core.

Upon landing on the rugged shoreline, Belen folded her

wings and cast her eyes around, fully expecting to be greeted—or challenged—by sentinels. Sure enough, the guardians of the island soon appeared, their eyes scrutinizing her as if trying to peer into her very soul. After a brief but intense exchange, they led her toward the Temple of Foresight.

As Belen walked through the corridors of the temple, she sensed eyes upon her, each gaze a fleeting touch, yet no one spoke. Could they sense the emotional maelstrom within her, the torment that stabbed at her with every step? She had to fight the urge to roar, to confront them with the rawness of her pain. But she held it in, her jaw clenched in anticipation.

Her escorts led her to a dimly lit chamber, its atmosphere heavy with the scent of ancient incense. Before a dancing flame sat a blue dragon, her eyes shrouded by a hood. At her side was an imposing winged canine, which lifted its head and pricked its ears as Belen approached.

"Sister," Chandra murmured softly, turning her hooded face toward Belen.

At the sight of Chandra, Belen's heart stuttered in her chest, a swell of conflicting emotions surging through her. Anger and betrayal gnawed at her soul. Chandra had foretold her great loss, a prophecy that ushered her into her role as the Jade Empress. So why had there been no prophecy about the attack that shattered her Court? Her eyes narrowed, their emerald glow dimming with her rising bitterness, as she took measured steps toward the hooded dragon.

"I *trusted* you," Belen's voice was a venomous whisper, each word dripping with accusation and barely restrained fury. "Why did you not forewarn me of the assault on my Court?"

Chandra sighed and stood up, turning to face Belen. "I did warn you, sister. But you chose to ignore my words."

Belen's wings flared out in anger. The tips of her talons bit into the stone floor. "Ignore your words? You told me that I would suffer a great loss, not that my entire Court would be destroyed! Not that I would lose my mate!"

The white canine's upper lip curled in a silent warning, a flash of fangs. Belen was tempted to swipe at the beast, just to have an outlet for her renewed anger.

Chandra lifted a claw to stroke the canine's silky head. "Peace, Vesper. I couldn't prevent the attack, Belen. It was part of the path we were on, ultimately leading to your rise as the Jade Empress."

Belen's voice shook as she spoke. "But at what cost, Chandra? My family is gone, my Court is in ruins! How can you stand there and say this was meant to be?"

Chandra hesitated, her hooded gaze shifting to the floor. "There are some things I cannot change, Belen. I cannot control the course of fate."

Fate. Belen hated winds-cursed fate. She refused to be its pawn any longer. "Tell me everything, Chandra. How did this happen? Why did the drakes turn against us?"

The Seer heaved a long, whistling sigh. "I believe you know why."

Belen mantled her wings, baring her fangs. "I was going to help them when I became Empress!"

Chandra nodded. "And now you are. So what will you do? What path have you taken?"

"We killed all the drakes left at the Jade Court," Belen growled, passion rich in her voice. "I took the path of vengeance. Of honoring the memory of my mate and the previous Emperor and Empress."

"Do you really believe all that death honors them, or will it lead to a cycle of hate?" Chandra asked.

Belen bristled. How dare Chandra question her? "It's *very* easy to stand on the outside and judge my actions. You have lost nothing."

Chandra shook her head. "No, I've lost my sister. And I will mourn that for the rest of my days."

"You can't mourn someone who's not dead," Belen shot back. "Betray, though? You can most certainly do that."

The Seer shivered, her azure scales chiming. "I'm sorry," Chandra said softly. "This is the path we must take, Belen. I know it's hard and I wish it could be different, but all other paths would have led to far worse outcomes."

"There are worse things than this pain I feel?" Belen snapped, her tail lashing. "Than losing my mate? Losing the dragons of a Court?"

"I know it sounds–"

Before Chandra could utter another word, Belen's claws were a blur of movement, slashing across the blue dragon's face with a ferocity born of betrayal and anguish. Chandra gasped, her head jerking to the side under the impact, while her cheek wept with fresh, crimson slashes that stood out vividly against her scales.

Nearby, the winged canine growled menacingly, its ears pinned back against its skull. In response, Belen bared her fangs, her own snarl a warning that she was a tempest barely contained.

"Don't patronize me, Chandra. I thought I could trust you. Curse you and curse your visions. If you ever dare betray me again, I'll kill you."

And with her proclamation, Belen stormed out of the Temple of Foresight.

CHAPTER
FIFTEEN

Belen descended back to the Jade Court, her wings beating against the weight of conflicting emotions—anger and determination warring within her. As her talons touched the emerald-hued earth, a gust from her wings kicked up a mini cyclone of dust, whirling around her like a dance of chaos and purpose.

She walked into the heart of the Court, and as if summoned by her very presence, the surviving dragons encircled her. Their eyes met hers, each gaze a blend of awe and anticipation, as if she were the compass that would guide them out of their disarray.

Even the apex dragons and the colossal leviathans, once aloof, now looked at her with a reverence they had never before shown. It was as if the entire Court held its breath, waiting for her to speak, their silent entreaties adding to the gravity of the moment.

"I am your Empress," Belen declared, her voice unwavering. "Together, we will ensure the Jade Court is stronger than ever before. We will no longer rely on drakes, but on ourselves and our allies. This is a new beginning for us."

A murmur of approval rippled through the crowd of dragons. They had been through so much, but Belen's words seemed to offer them a sense of direction.

Belen cast a contemplative look toward the distant jungle, keenly aware that just beyond its leafy veil lay the beach—and buried in its sands, the delicate eggs that represented the Court's future. "As Empress, I will lead you through this darkness. We will find a way to survive this ordeal, I promise you that."

With the eyes of her Court upon her, Belen turned and scaled the stones leading to the Jade Dais. The Court watched in rapt attention, their collective gaze following her ascent. Once she reached the dais, she turned back to face them. Her tail whipped through the air as she stretched her neck skyward, and then came the roar—a seismic sound that filled the valley, echoing off its walls and etching itself into the very essence of the Jade Court.

The Court answered, their roars joining hers in a defiant chorus. Belen sucked in a deep breath, surveying the courtiers. It was intoxicating, but also humbling, a reminder of the incredible responsibility that now rested on her shoulders.

"I will make the difficult decisions and sacrifices necessary to keep our Court safe," Belen continued once the last roar died to silence. "And I will not rest until we have brought every last traitor to justice."

Cheers rose at her words. With fierce determination, Belen leaped down from the Jade Dais and landed in front of her Court. "We will not be defeated," she declared, her voice ringing out like a bell. "We will not be destroyed. We are the Jade Court!"

With her declaration resonating in the hearts of her Court,

Belen turned and unfurled her majestic wings, sweeping them in a grand arc to make way as she headed toward the nursery bower. An apex dragon, his scales the color of rich mahogany, fell in step behind her.

"With your permission, Empress, I wish to stand guard," he offered respectfully.

Belen smiled warmly and gave a nod that was as much an acknowledgment of his loyalty as it was a royal decree.

Upon reaching the beach, she found another apex dragon vigilantly positioned beside the nursery bower. Her eyes settled on the protective mound of sand and foliage that concealed her precious eggs. She exhaled softly, her breath a mix of relief and apprehension. These fragile shells held the future of the Jade Court, and every maternal fiber in her body told her that they would soon break open to reveal their treasure.

Belen kept a vigilant watch on the beach for days on end, guarding the future of her lineage and Court. The apex sentinels, understanding the gravity of her dual role, brought her nourishing meals—everything from ocean-fresh fish to succulent fruits.

Between caring for her eggs and meeting with advisors, Belen plotted out the next steps to protect her Court. As she engaged in a lively discourse with Miralda, the distinct sound of a cracking shell punctuated their conversation, followed by the soft, pleading chirp of new life.

"Ah, would you like to tend to your newborn?" Miralda paused, her eyes widening in anticipation.

Belen's eyes flickered toward the nursery bower. She had intentionally cleared its top so she could keep an eye on her eggs. "My young are strong and capable of hatching while we focus on pressing matters for the Court." She had heard the murmurs—that she would be too engrossed in motherhood to effectively rule. But Belen was committed to proving she could flawlessly do both.

"If that's what you wish," Miralda agreed, though her eyes were on the bower. "I would be happy to sit with the little ones..."

"The *Vangara*, Miralda," Belen said, keeping to the task at hand. "We were speaking of the Vangara."

"Right," the Councilor murmured, turning back to the Empress. "Look, I know you're eager to forge new alliances, but I don't know if the Vangara are a good match for the Jade Court."

Belen lifted her chin, eyes narrowing. But she heard another peep from the bower, and she couldn't help herself. She eased closer, peering inside to discover that one of her eggs had a long crack. A huge chunk of shell fell away from the egg, revealing a wet green snout and a bright eye. *Oh, the baby.* Belen swallowed, the urge to greet her firstborn too much to rein in. She leaned over, using a claw to crack the rest of the egg so she could scoop out the whelp.

"A male. Oh, if only Gideon were here to see you." Belen licked the top of the whelp's head, clearing away the liquid that had protected the youngster in the shell. Cuddling the whelp against her, she returned to their discussion. "The Vangara oppose the drakes. That's why I selected them, Miralda."

The older dragoness grimaced. "But they're..." She shivered her wings. "Freakish. Unsightly, even."

Miralda wasn't wrong. Drakes and the Vangara were both close relatives of the dragons—offshoots that had come about due to a magical disaster centuries ago. The drakes had become smaller, with soft scales and a gift of magic. The Vangara had shriveled into bipedal dragons without working wings, creatures that seemed to survive out of sheer spite. Seen as nightmarish horrors, the Vangara had retreated to a chain of islands south of the Dragon Latitudes.

"The perfect allies against the drakes," Belen insisted. After being twisted by magic, the Vangara hated it—and thus, hated the drakes, their antithesis.

Miralda sighed. "We'll send an emissary, if that's truly your wish. But don't say I didn't tell you so if this causes an uprising."

Belen smiled. "See that it's done, Miralda. Now if you'll excuse me, I wish to spend time with my newborn son. He requires food." The hungry whelp was nibbling on the scales at her shoulder.

Mention of the whelp softened the Councilor. Miralda gave an indulgent smile. "Of course. I'll have someone bring a fat rabbit for the little one. Perhaps a mango to gnaw on."

Belen watched the dragoness go, then turned back to the whelp. He watched her with lambent eyes. "Your father lives on through you, so you will bear his name. Welcome to the Jade Court, Gideon." She nuzzled the whelp, breathing out a contented breath.

With little Gideon chirping in hunger, Belen breathed out a contented sigh. She *would* secure the future of the Jade Court. Lead them into a new era of strength and prosperity.

And no one would dare stand in her way.

CHAPTER SIXTEEN

Asher

Asher's wings strained against the gale that threatened to blow him off course. He plowed onward, determined to reach the Vault of Fate. It was his last, best chance at uncovering a way to strike at the heart of the Jade Court.

The sting of defeat still fresh, Asher mulled over the calamitous toll of their ill-fated strike. Humans and drakes alike had fallen, and their numbers had dwindled drastically. Some of the humans, their spirits broken and faces etched with terror, had even fled the scene in the *Revenant*, the airship that had once symbolized their collective hope.

In the pit of his stomach, a gnawing realization had taken hold. It was only a matter of time before Belen, the new Jade Empress, would marshal her forces to hunt down what remained of his tattered rebellion.

He was determined to make certain she never had the chance.

As Asher approached the formidable structure of the Vault of Fate, his senses were on high alert. Each beat of his wings was measured, cautious. A dragon sentinel emerged to intercept him. The sentinel scrutinized Asher, its gaze piercing yet dispassionate.

After Asher revealed his purpose—to consult the Seer—the sentinel wordlessly gestured for him to follow and led him into the Temple of Foresight.

Asher took a deep breath, finally allowing himself to relax. The knots of tension that had clenched his muscles began to unravel, and he felt lighter than he had in days. It was as if the temple itself were granting him a brief respite from the struggles that awaited him outside its walls.

"Seer, a drake to see you," the dragon announced.

Asher peered around his escort to find a dark blue dragoness resting on a balcony that overlooked the lush island. She wore a hood over her head, but still, she turned in his direction. She breathed out a soft sigh.

"Ah, yes. I foresaw your arrival." The Seer rose, stretching with the motion. A big white dog Asher hadn't noticed clambered to his feet on the dragon's far side. No, wait, that wasn't a dog–it was an aralez, a legendary canine known for flight and the healing properties of its saliva.

Asher cleared his throat. "Greetings, Seer. If you saw my arrival, then you know why I've come."

"Chandra," the dragoness said. "You may call me Chandra. And I know why you are here." She heaved another great sigh, as if something pained her. The Seer flicked her claws at the sentinel. "You are dismissed."

The azure dragon waited until the other dragon was gone. The aralez whined, licking his mistress's cheek when she lowered her head.

"The path you are on was forged long ago, and it will only

be broken by another cycle of loss," Chandra murmured, stepping closer.

Asher frowned. That made little sense to him. "We made a bid against the Jade Court and lost."

"Everyone lost." Chandra's voice was a heavy-hearted whisper. "I know you seek freedom. The price is high."

"Freedom is worth any cost," Asher shot back.

He felt as if she gave him a nebulous look from beneath her hood. "There are times I wonder if that is true." The Seer shook her head.

Asher clenched his claws until the tips bit into his flesh. "We're too deep in this to back down. I know these dragons. They won't rest until we're dead—not after what we did."

"On that count, you are right." Chandra rocked from side to side, as if considering her next words. "The dragons are uniting under their new Empress. But there is a way... a way to weaken them and make them vulnerable."

Asher leaned in, his ears straining to catch her every word. "Tell me, please."

"The dragon fruits," the Seer whispered. "They are the key. You have a drake capable of manipulating plants."

Asher swallowed. Macawi. Did he dare commit her to this plan? But it might be the only way. He would make sure she wasn't in it alone. "Yes."

Chandra turned, facing the view. In the distance, a bird chittered. "There is a way she can taint the fruit. The dragons won't taste a difference if she does it correctly. But over time, the blight will strike the dragons and make their wings wither, stripping them of flight."

Asher's eyes widened. He had entertained fantasies of binding the dragons to the ground by tearing off their wings, but they were just that—fantasies. Not even his golems had accomplished such a feat in the heat of battle.

"It can't be that easy," he said.

Chandra gave him a sad smile. "It's not easy. This is another step down a path from which you cannot return."

"We've been committed to this path for a while," Asher said.

"Yes," Chandra whispered, and there was a frisson of pain in her voice. It struck Asher as odd, but he was too distracted with thoughts of what he and Macawi must accomplish. Grounding the Jade Court once and for all would guarantee the safety of the remaining drakes.

"Thank you for your advice, Seer," Asher said, bowing his head to her.

"Do not thank me for this," Chandra murmured, agony wrapped in each word. She paused, her head whipping around to him. "One more thing."

Asher tilted his head. "Yes?"

"The eggs. Your eggs," Chandra murmured. "Hide them well."

Asher's gut clenched at the request. "What do you know, Seer?"

She shook her head. "I can't tell you, or we'll be sent spiraling down an even worse path."

The drake flared his nostrils. If he weren't half her size and outnumbered by dragons on this island, he might find a way to intimidate her. But he'd have to settle for a plea. "If it means my whelps might suffer, I need to know."

The tip of Chandra's tail twitched. "I can't tell you much, but if you hide your eggs well, I can see them down the path. Two fine drakes. One copper, one opal."

Asher smiled, unable to hide his pride. A whelp that would have his pale coloring, and another that would favor Macawi's copper. They sounded wonderful, and he couldn't wait to meet them. "We'll hide them."

Chandra regarded him for a moment before nodding in satisfaction. "Good. Remember, the future is not set in stone. It is always changing, always in motion." She paused, as if waiting for him to say something. When he remained silent, she continued. "Be careful, Asher. There are forces at play that even I cannot predict."

Asher nodded, his thoughts heavy with the weight of Chandra's words.

Chandra turned to the aralez. "Come, my friend. We have much to do." And then in a surprise to Asher, she took off from the balcony, though the flying canine took the lead, as if he were guiding her.

As the Seer flew off, Asher stood there a moment longer, lost in thought. He knew what he had to do. He had to make sure that Macawi was on board with this plan, and that they both saw it through to the end. It was their only chance to strike back against the Jade Court, and to ensure a future for their children.

With newfound determination, Asher turned and made his way out of the Temple of Foresight, ready to take on whatever lay ahead. He and his mate were a force to be reckoned with, and the dragons of the Jade Court would soon learn just how fierce their resolve truly was.

CHAPTER SEVENTEEN

"For the last time, I promise you, they're safe," Asher whispered as he and Macawi landed on the farthest tip of Jadefire Island, in an area he hoped was far from the prying eyes of the dragon sentries. The full moon overhead illuminated the cresting waves around them.

"How are you so certain?" Macawi demanded, her eyes flashing as she changed from drake into the slender form of a woman. She crossed her arms. "How are you so trusting this dragon Seer will assure the safety of our eggs?"

"Because she's not a part of any Court," Asher said, assuming his own human form. In these smaller shapes, it would be even more difficult for the dragons to spot them. "And it's hard to explain, but the Seer was...she was insistent about keeping the eggs safe. I told you she saw them down the path."

The copper drake sighed. "You did. I just wish I could believe it. I'll feel better about this when the task is done and we're back on the island with our eggs." She swallowed. They both knew that in a matter of days, the eggs would hatch. Soon they would meet their children.

Asher slung an arm around her. "Then let's hurry and get this done and be back with them, hmm?" He pressed his lips to her forehead.

Macawi leaned into him before pulling away. "Let's go. Try to keep up." As graceful as a butterfly, Macawi dashed into the darkness.

Oh, it would be perfect if this were simply a lark and not a life-and-death situation. Chin tucked, Asher raced after her, his keen eyes never leaving the bob of auburn hair on his mate's head.

"Macawi! Hold!" Asher hissed when he saw a dozen dark shapes take to the wing over the island. The female drake slid to a stop beneath the eerie limbs of a banyan tree.

Asher joined her, and together they watched as the dragons circled the island once before heading to the west. The way he and Macawi had come.

"What do you think they're doing?" Macawi's voice was a breathy whisper.

He shook his head. "No idea. But this can only be good for us...that's twelve less dragons to worry about."

"I counted at least three apexes and two leviathans in that group," Macawi murmured. "You know it's unheard of for them to hunt together."

But not unheard of for them to fight together. Asher clenched his jaw. "Come on."

The pair continued onward, slipping through the jungle until they reached the dragon fruit grove. The dragon fruit trees looked odd compared to the other flora on the island, reminiscent more of a strange cactus than a proper tree. The long, spiky branches reminded him of a dragon's tail–even more so with the bulbous fruits attached to the ends.

Macawi paused, hands on her hips as she surveyed the grove. The dragon fruits were a favorite of the Jade Court, though they had a hallucinogenic effect and were usually saved for special occasions, or used as medicine.

As Asher watched, his mate knelt beside the nearest tree, placing her hand flat against the trunk. Macawi shut her eyes in concentration. Asher didn't know exactly what she did, but moments later her eyes flashed open again.

"I figured it out. I only need to make a connection with a few more and they will pass it from one to another, like an illness," she whispered, slipping over to the next tree.

"And then from the fruits, to the dragons themselves?" Asher asked.

"Yes."

Asher squinted at the first tree she had touched. He didn't notice anything different about it. He brushed his fingertips against the trunk.

"Give me some credit. You won't find any traces of what I did," Macawi hissed, annoyance in her voice.

He nodded. "So I see. Or rather, don't see."

After what felt like an eternity, Macawi stepped back, her face weary but triumphant. "It's done." Her voice was strained with exhaustion.

Pride surged through Asher. Surely he had the cleverest and bravest mate among all drakes. He reached for her hand, giving it a reassuring squeeze. "You did amazing, my love. Now let's—"

A roar of alarm cut him off. "Intruders!"

"Oh guano," Macawi murmured, her eyes wide.

Asher bit back a growl of frustration, then pushed her ahead of him. "Go. Shift and fly. I'll keep them off your tail."

"But—"

He shook his head. "Go!"

Asher turned, listening to the sound of his mate's retreating steps. He crouched down, digging his fingers into the soil, his nexus chain warm against his chest. Though he had been away from Jadefire Island for months, he still knew it from years of living there. And the stone of the island knew him—he had bled upon it, and that held great power.

The dragon sentry charged up, eyes bright in the moonlight. Fangs bared and glistening. In his human form, Asher was a tiny mite compared to the incoming behemoth.

"A human!" the dragon roared. "You'll die now."

Asher smiled, rising and lifting his hands.

The sides of the valley rumbled as two huge veins pulled free from either side. The dragon slowed at the unexpected sight. Sweat beaded Asher's forehead, and already his skull pounded from the sheer size of the construct he was commanding.

The twin arms of stone swung down, slamming into the dragon.

The sentry never had a chance, crushed beneath ton upon ton of rock. As soon as the dragon went down, Asher released his hold on the stone. He swayed on his feet, then shook his head.

"Drake!" The voice was familiar, full of command. Asher looked up and discovered the Jade Consort hovering overhead. No, not Consort...she would be the Empress now. Belen dove at him.

Asher turned and ran.

The emerald dragoness was fast, but he was small, capable of getting through twisted trunks of trees that required her to fly over or around. Belen roared her fury. Heart pounding, Asher plowed onward, his lungs burning. If he was going to get out of this alive, he needed a plan.

He couldn't take Belen alone, as much as he wished it. Especially not after exhausting his magic. No, he simply needed the Jade Empress to leave him alone. Better still, to think him dead, so she would never have a reason to come after him again.

With a grim smile, an idea formed. Winds, if this went wrong it would be his end...but it might not matter. Asher ran for the treacherous east end of the island, where years ago a sinkhole had opened up. Most of the dragons and drakes had avoided it since it could be a death trap even for a creature with wings.

Feet slapping against the dirt, he ran onward, arms pumping at his sides. Belen flew overhead. Asher's eyes narrowed as his magic told him he drew near his destination. He just had to bolt across a broad clearing where the Jade Empress would have ample opportunity to snag him.

Asher drew to a stop at the edge of the clearing, watching as the Empress looped, preparing to land. Yeah, he had to get to the sinkhole before she got in his way. By the four winds, he wished he could stop for rest. But if he did, he was dead.

He bolted into the clearing, running as fast as he could.

Belen shrieked her fury.

Almost there. So close.

The green dragon dove at him.

The sinkhole spread before him, a black gaping maw. Asher jumped.

Belen's talons missed him by a hands' breadth.

The drake fell into the darkness, fighting the urge to scream as he called on the last remnants of his magic before he hit the unforgiving ground...

A stone fist snatched him, slowing his fall and dumping him to the ground.

It still hurt, but he didn't die. Asher lay on his back, staring at the blackness overhead. He heard Belen's angry roars and curses.

"You denied me my vengeance, coward!" Bits of stone clattered as it fell down, a sign that the Empress must be pacing around the crater. Was she going to try to come down? Surely she wasn't foolish. Finally, she yelled, "I'll celebrate your death!"

With her pronouncement, Asher settled back with a sigh, catching his breath. He was safe, for the moment. When he had time to recover, he hoped his magic would help him get out.

And it did, though it took longer than he liked to recover. Half a day, in fact. But eventually, he took his drake form and using claws and magic, scaled the sinkhole. When he reached the top, he peered out, surveying his surroundings before crawling out. He shook off a layer of grime, then took to the air on a roundabout course he hoped would help him catch up with Macawi.

CHAPTER
EIGHTEEN

With every beat of his wings, Asher willed himself to go faster, cutting through the sky as though chased by the Fates themselves. Macawi and their unborn were his beacon, the source of his desperate flight towards Dead Man's Dare. But as the island's contours emerged on the horizon, thick, acrid smoke spiraled upwards, staining the sky a sinister black. A guttural sense of dread seized him, suffocating his earlier hope. He flapped his wings harder, each beat an exclamation of fear for what lay ahead

The moment Asher's claws touched the sands of Dead Man's Dare, the grim reality shattered any remnants of hope. The air was tainted with the smell of burning wood and flesh. Before him unfolded a tableau of sheer horror.

A human woman ran, screaming, from town with a leviathan on her heels. As Asher watched, the monster reared over her, jaws gaping. A scissoring clash of fangs cut off the woman's terrified shriek.

Macawi. My children. Where are they?

Equal parts fear and anger flooding his veins, Asher raced toward the settlement. He had to find Macawi. Had to get the eggs—

Suddenly, he spotted his mate amidst the chaos, her copper scales glinting in the firelight. She was locked in a fierce battle with one of the invading dragons, her slender form dodging and weaving as she fought with all her strength. The dragon wasn't the largest of the bunch—only twice her size—but she was still outmatched.

A roar built in his chest. As tired as he was, he couldn't let her fall. He surged forward to rush to her aid—

A dragon slammed into him, sending him skidding painfully into the side of a ruined building. He shook himself as he staggered to his feet, only to find another of the dragons towering over him.

"Asher!" Macawi's cry snared the attention of the dragon, too. "Get out of here! The eggs—"

Her words were stripped away as the dragon turned on her. She was caught between her previous attacker and the new one. The copper drake didn't stand a chance.

In the narrow space between the two dragons, he caught her pleading gaze. He didn't want to leave her. Not like this. He was not a coward.

"Go!" she called again. "The drakes...our future...needs you."

The dragons fell on her, all clashing fangs and tearing claws. Macawi screamed.

It took everything he had to turn tail and flee. As he took to the air, another of the dragons lumbered into the sky to chase him. As he flew for all he was worth, his heart twisted with grief at the sickening feeling of abandoning his mate and their unborn children to a terrible fate. The realization weighed heavily upon him, a relentless reminder of his perceived failure. Consumed by sorrow, he vowed that he would find a way to make things right, even if it took centuries.

CHAPTER NINETEEN

Belen

Belen stood on the highest peak of Jadefire Island, her emerald scales gleaming in the sun as she surveyed her domain. The scent of smoke and burning wood drifted to her on the west wind, a testament to the power and fury of the Jade Court. A grim sense of satisfaction filled her with the hope that those that had dared to attack the Jade Court had now paid the price for their folly.

As the dragons returned to the island, they regaled her with tales of the devastation they had unleashed on the unsuspecting settlements. Their voices were filled with pride and excitement, but there was also a dark undertone of bloodlust. They had enjoyed the hunt and destruction. Belen couldn't fault them, not after the pain they had endured.

Little Gideon, her first-hatched whelp, skittered up to her as Belen alighted in the valley. His brothers and sisters tumbled around, all awkward wings and stubby claws as they playfully growled at one another. Miralda watched them, appearing relaxed though Belen knew the Councilor was a fierce protector.

"Time for the feast, little ones," Belen murmured, lowering her head to rub her muzzle against Gideon. The whelp batted at her with a playful claw, giggling as he fell onto his side in a ball. The other whelps dashed over, crowding around.

"You have done well," Miralda said, rising to join them. Together, they made their way to the dragon fruit grove, where the rest of the courtiers had gathered in preparation.

Someone had set the younger dragons to collecting the fruit, and they were gathered in huge baskets all around the clearing. The vibrant pink and green orbs were a delicacy, their sweet, juicy flesh intoxicating to the senses. Belen could hardly wait to savor them. But first...

"Dragons of the Jade Court, today we celebrate victory over those who sought to tear us down," she declared. They roared in celebration. "And today, we will remember those we lost, even as we look forward to a brighter future." Belen couldn't help but glance down at her whelps as she spoke. "Feast, and listen as our warriors regale us with stories of their strike against our foes."

As the dragons ate, their eyes took on a glazed, unfocused look, a sign that the hallucinogenic effects of the fruit were taking hold. They laughed and wove on their feet, tongues and inhibitions loosening.

Belen watched her subjects with a mixture of pride and concern, acutely aware that their recent acts of destruction had pushed them further towards the brink of chaos. The loss of the former Jade monarchs and the betrayal of the drakes had taken its toll on the once-proud and noble dragons. She knew she needed to bring them back from the edge, but the path forward was uncertain.

One of the dragons, a leviathan with scales as dark as

obsidian, approached Belen, his enormous form casting a long shadow over the grove. "My Empress," he rumbled, his voice deep and gravelly. "The human settlements have been razed to the ground, and our enemies have been vanquished. We have avenged our fallen Emperor." He staggered on his feet and belched before laughing as if he had spouted forth the most clever joke.

Belen inclined her head, acknowledging the leviathan's words. "You have done well, my loyal subjects. But we cannot rest on our laurels; there is much to be done to ensure the safety and prosperity of our Court."

The other dragons, their bellies full of dragon fruit, murmured their agreement, their voices echoing through the grove like the rumble of distant thunder. As Belen gazed at the sea of faces turned towards her, the sheer magnitude of her duty was humbling.

"Let this feast mark the beginning of a new era for the Jade Court," she declared, her voice strong and unwavering. "We will rise from the ashes of our losses and rebuild our legacy. We will show the world that we are not to be trifled with."

The dragons roared their approval, the sound resonating through the air and shaking the very ground beneath their feet. As the echoes of their cries faded into the distance, Belen looped her tail around Gideon, pulling the whelp close. He protested with a shrill peep before tumbling against her, content. Not to be left out, Gideon's siblings swarmed. The whelps fell into a giggling tangle.

A new era, indeed.

CHAPTER
TWENTY

Miralda's footsteps were hesitant, almost reluctant, as she approached Belen. Her face was a mask of grave concern. "Another of the apexes has lost her wings," she reported in a hushed, quivering voice, her head lowered in a gesture of deference and sadness.

Belen shut her eyes, as if trying to will away the reality of Miralda's words. A heavy sigh escaped her maw. "This is turning into a nightmare," she murmured.

In the weeks that had passed since the celebratory feast, an air of unease had settled over the Jade Court. Once resplendent and powerful, dragons of all sizes were now afflicted by an inexplicable malady. Their wings, once symbols of their might and freedom, were deteriorating—withering away as if consumed by an invisible fire.

Whispers of fear and panic coursed through the Court like a raging river, threatening to engulf them all. Belen's heart ached as she watched her dragons struggle to fly, their once-graceful forms now clumsily flapping through the air. The dragons that had once ruled the skies were now grounded, and the pride of the Jade Court was in danger of being crushed beneath the weight of their despair.

And worst of all, Belen herself was not immune to the horror. She stared straight ahead, unwilling to spare a glance at her own tattered wings. The membrane had been the first to go, thinning and developing painful holes that no balm could remedy. Then the bones of the wings themselves developed an awful radiating pain, as if they were being eaten away from the inside.

It had taken longer than Belen liked for them to figure out that the culprit was the dragon fruit. By then, every single dragon—even the youngest, including her precious whelps—had eaten of the fruits. Now Belen feared she would lose her children, and she didn't know how to fix any of this.

"Empress?" Miralda prodded.

"I heard."

"We must do something," Miralda implored. "The dragons are losing hope, and our power is dwindling. We cannot allow this to continue."

Belen looked at her trusted advisor, her heart heavy with the burden of her people's suffering. "I know, Miralda. But what can we do? We have searched for answers, but none have been found."

"We received word that the Vangara agreed to the terms of an alliance," the orange dragon said after a moment, shifting uncomfortably.

Belen's eyes widened. At last, a bit of good news. She was so weary, it should have invigorated her, but it didn't. No, inside she felt as hollow and withered as her wings. As if her heart had shriveled up and died. The Vangara, a martial people, would be strong allies in this time of crisis. But her dragons needed more than that. They needed hope. Freedom; and that had been stripped with the destruction of their wings.

Unless...

"We need the skies," Belen whispered.

Miralda canted her head, uncertain. She glanced at her own bedraggled wings. "Empress? Are you well?"

Belen choked back a laugh. None of them were well, not a single one. But they would be, in time. She would make sure of that.

"When the Vangara emissary arrives, we will make plans," Belen began, moving to pace around her lair. Her whelps, weakened from their normally rambunctious state, lifted their heads to watch her. "They have experience in the human world."

"The human world?" Miralda repeated, eyes widening.

Belen nodded. "We have riches. Humans like the precious metals and gems we hoard."

"The metals we can no longer harvest for our own scales!" Miralda argued, alarmed. "All we have left here...there will be a metal famine. It's not enough."

"I'm thinking of the long term," Belen continued, fire rising in her veins as the plan formed. Everyone else was so short-sighted. Had always been so blasted short-sighted, preparing for an hour from now when they needed to be thinking in terms of years. Decades, even. "We'll have the Vangara act as brokers to help us secure an airship."

"What?" Miralda's jaw dropped, revealing gleaming fangs.

"We will reclaim the skies on our own terms," Belen whispered, moving over to Gideon and picking him up tenderly in her claws. "We will not be defeated by the loss of our wings. We will find a cure, and we will rise once more."

And, Belen vowed deep in her heart, she would strike down any remaining drakes who crossed her path...after she had tortured information about the wing-blight from them, anyway.

She was the Jade Empress, and she would not be broken by this. Belen would restore the Jade Court to its former glory and see justice done.

No matter the cost.

The story continues in *Dragon Latitudes*!

Also by Amy Campbell

Tales of the Outlaw Mages

Breaker

Effigest

Dreamer

Persuader

Songbinder

Airship Dragons

Dragon Latitudes

Manufactured by Amazon.ca
Bolton, ON